PERSONS UNKNOWN

PERSONS UNKNOWN

Gwen Moffat

C

CHIVERS LARGE PRINT
BATH

British Library Cataloguing in Publication Data available

This Large Print edition published by Chivers Press, Bath, 2001.

Published by arrangement with the author.

U.K. Hardcover ISBN 0 7540 4379 7

Photoset, printed and bound in Great Britain by
Redwood Books, Trowbridge, Wiltshire

PERSONS UNKNOWN

CHAPTER ONE

'I HAD A dream,' old Roderick said with heavy drama, and waited for his housekeeper to register interest.

'Let's get you sitting up first.'

Iris MacNally set down his breakfast tray and advanced on the bed: a big solid woman in a dress that had seen better days.

Roderick glared at her. 'Keep yer hands off me, woman! I can sit up on me own, *and* I'm finished with breakfast in bed. I've never in the whole of me life—'

'You've been having it in bed for three days now. The doctor said you'd got to watch your—'

'He's a bloody quack!' The old man was covered by nothing heavier than a sheet but the effort to sit up unaided was beyond his strength. Wincing, he sank back on his pillows.

'You see,' she said without triumph, 'you can still do with a hand. You've strained those muscles and they've got to tone up gradually; no sense in trying to hurry Nature.'

'Damme, Iris!' She helped him into a sitting position and he drooped over his knees: a

1

fierce little figure bristling at his own inadequacy. Iris plumped the pillows and eased him back with a large hand. He perked up at this and his eyes gleamed balefully.

'You're enjoying this. Yer like having me in bed, don't yer?'

'It's for your own good, Mr Bowen.'

'I'm getting up today.'

'Of course you are: after lunch; you can sit by the window and watch your birds—'

'I'm getting up after breakfast. It's me birthday.'

'There! You took the words right out of my mouth as I came in the door. You and your old dreams.' She had an accent which she might have termed refined but with traces of Liverpool and Ireland lurking in the corners. 'Many happy returns of the day, Mr Bowen, and if you'll only look after yourself properly, I'm sure there'll be many more of the same.' She beamed comfortably at him.

'And I want champagne.'

'I'll be seeing to it.'

'With me breakfast.'

'Aren't you a one? Now, here's your tea; look: why don't I throw out this awful old mug? It's cracked all—'

'Where's me bacon?'

'The fat's bad for your heart.'

'Jesus Christ! You're always saying people are as old as they feel. I'm eighty-seven today and I feel like a two-year-old—organically.' He looked evil. 'And that don't mean what you think it means. It's all very well for you to primp yer mouth, but young men have falls too; I've been in a lot worse state than this in me time: broken bones into the bargain.' His eyes glazed. 'That time I came off the Breithorn I broke the femur in one leg, the tibia in the other, in *two* places. I was lying on the glacier for eight hours before they found me.'

'Gracious. You could have died of pneumonia.'

'Pneumonia, woman? Don't be soft. It's exposure in the Alps: what they call hypothermia these days. Kept meself alive by controlled shivering. Painful business: I could hear those broken bones grating together.'

'Now, now, Mr Bowen.'

He grinned happily. 'Kept passing out from shock. Not much pain, yer see; when it got too bad, I passed out again. Quite a good night really. I wasn't alone at the end.'

'I'm sure you weren't.'

'Ha! Not in *that* way. This was some chap who came and sat with me, near me, just out of the corner of me eye: out of focus, I mean. Comfortable sort of feller.'

3

'Did he say anything?'

'Not a word. They don't, yer know. He just kept me company until the rescuers arrived. Quite a common occurrence in the mountains, specially when you're a bit under the weather. You wouldn't understand, of course. You've led a sheltered life.'

'Now you're teasing.'

'So I know what serious injury's like, which is more than you do, for all you've set yerself up as me nurse. And I'm just bruised this time. You're fussing like an old hen.'

'You're black and blue all down one side, and you've had a very nasty shock.'

He put down his mug with deliberation.

'Anyone would be shocked at an attempt on his life.'

'Anyone,' Iris said serenely, 'would be shocked at falling fifteen feet down the granary steps.'

'I was pushed!'

She crossed to the window and picked up a vase of tiger lilies. 'These don't last long in the heat. I'll pick some fresh.'

'Don't trouble.'

'You don't like lilies?'

'They're all right for funerals. What's this on me cereal?'

'It's some of Rachel's bran.'

4

'Horse fodder! And me bowels are me own business. I'm coming down for me bacon.'

'Mr Bowen! If you'll only stay in bed while I give the doctor a ring. You're my responsibility, you're putting me in a very awkward—'

Her voice rose as the door opened. A young man with thick blond hair looked in.

'What's going on here? Many happy returns of the day, Rod.'

'Norman! Thank you, me boy. This bloody woman's bullying me again.'

'Mr Bowen!'

'Stop laying down the law, Iris; it's his birthday. How're you feeling, Rod?'

'Fit as a flea, lad. I'm getting up.'

'You do that. We'll go for a swim. Work the stiffness out of the muscles.'

'The doctor said—'

'Mr Bowen knows what's best for him, Iris, and he's got a constitution like an ox. I'll help you dress, Rod.'

The two men exchanged glances. Iris backed to the door. 'I wash my hands of it, Mr Bowen; I'm only thinking of what's best for you . . . and your own family have got no call to encourage you.' She sniffed furiously, her hands rolling her apron. 'You shouldn't employ me if you don't trust me. You know

5

it's for your own good. The doctor said—'

'You're employed as a housekeeper,' Roderick shouted as she opened the door, 'you ring that quack and you're fired!'

The door closed behind her. 'Damn woman!' He sank back against the pillows, exhausted. 'Lot of fuss about a bruise.'

'It was a bad fall, Rod.'

'I was *pushed*, lad.'

Norman sighed. 'You trod on a branch.'

'And where did the branch come from?'

'It fell off the tree.'

'There—was—no—wind.' It was like a ritual exchange—which it had become over the last few days.

'Branches can come down at any time.' Norman sounded tired. 'In this heat anything can happen.'

Roderick poked at his cereal. 'I had a dream,' he repeated hopefully.

The other sat down on the edge of the bed. 'Go on; I like your dreams.'

The old man had found his audience. He closed his eyes, concentrating on the picture in his mind. 'The peninsula was covered with enormous structures: cooling towers, and those things like outsize balls, covered with 'em so you couldn't see a blade of grass; all made of aluminium and gleaming in the

6

sun. And there was this pile near the middle, must have been sited right on the cromlech meadow. I was looking down on it all, a hawk's eye view from the fort, and I felt the earth tremble as if something under the ground was waking up and turning over and rousing itself . . . and the building on the cromlech meadow started to crumble, like a quarry face after the shot's fired. Then there were flames and the noise of an explosion and the whole bloody complex disintegrated: from Riffli Head right back to where Corn Farm once stood. White smoke, Norman, rising and, you know, that awful mushroom cloud?'

'It's all over, Rod.'

'And it went rolling up into an absolutely clear blue sky, folding over and over, and then the cloud started to move eastwards. . . .'

'We've all become obsessed with it, but stop worrying: you and Rachel together; you'll drive yourselves round the bend. We won, old chap! They chose another site.'

'You know why the first building collapsed?'

'Why?'

'They'd built it on the cromlech meadow.'

'Oh, I see. The—the Longheads objected.'

Roderick darted a glance at him from under jutting brows. 'There are more things

7

in heaven and earth, lad; don't forget that.'

'I'm not arguing—but I wish you'd forget the other side.'

'You're suggesting I forget a fast breeder reactor?' The tone was honeyed.

'They're not coming here, Rod.'

'Huh!'

'Well, isn't that what we're celebrating today? It's not only your eighty-seventh birthday—'

'Eighty-eighth.'

'Have it your way. It's the defeat of the Atomic Energy Authority as well. Hell, Rod; how many chaps of your age have taken on the Establishment and won?'

'Not me, lad; all of us.'

'But you spear-headed the Action Committee. It's your land.'

'Ah, yes. My land.' Roderick turned his head to the open window and for a moment they listened to the pigeons crooning in the woods. 'Family land.' He passed a thin hand over his skull. 'Right back to the Old People and on—by way of you and Rachel. Posterity: that's what it's all about.' He looked at his grandson-in-law with affection. 'I can't tell you how relieved I am that she found a feller with the same feeling for Riffli. . . . Strange how it can skip a generation; her father doesn't care.'

'Now, that's just not true; he's built that pub up into a flourishing business.'

'His wife has. Rupert's content to let her run it while he hobnobs with the customers and takes them out on trips to frighten the puffins in the nesting season.'

'So what? A good hotel needs a strong frontman. Doreen's far too busy behind the scenes to chat up the guests. Rupert's the P.R. man.'

'What's that? I don't hold with all these abbreviations.'

'Public Relations.'

'He's that all right.' The tone was gloomy rather than spiteful.

'So he's the ideal chap for the hotel. And up here you've got Rachel—who'll get stuck into the farming side when—when it's necessary—and she's got the same respect as you for the ancient places—no, I'm not laughing, I'm dead serious—and she's all for conserving the wildlife. And then again: Rupert and Doreen virtually run the village and they look after the holiday cottages which are beneath your notice despite the nice fat rents they bring in. What have you got to grumble about?'

'Lack of respect for one thing. Nice fat

9

rents indeed! You make me sound like an absentee landlord. Let me tell you: all that money goes straight back in the estate; there's no profit anywhere, not with the taxmen hanging on my tail like a crowd of vultures. I'm not grumbling. I was just saying: I'm glad Rachel married you; you're a lad after me own heart, and you—yer get on well, don't yer?' He held the other's eye.

'She's adorable.'

'Yes. Well.' The old fellow looked doubtfully at his tray. 'Funny dream,' he mused, 'Didn't know I had enemies . . . like that.'

'Who was the enemy in your dream?'

'In the dream? No, no. I was thinking about the branch on the granary steps.'

*   *   *

Norman came in the kitchen with Roderick's breakfast tray to find his wife and Iris Mac-Nally washing dishes at the sink. Rachel Kemp was nineteen: a plain girl with the big Bowen nose and a lot of tawny hair. There were dark circles under her deepset eyes.

'I'll go up to him now.' She dried her hands. 'How is he? Iris says he's being awkward.'

'He's muddled.' Her husband was munch-

10

ing a piece of toast from the tray. 'He's getting his dreams confused with reality—or what he takes for reality.'

'How?'

'Oh, dreaming about an atomic cloud over the peninsula and the Enemy at the top of the granary steps.'

Rachel grimaced at the housekeeper. 'Is he still shocked?'

'Could be.' The older woman was unperturbed. 'The fall was only three days ago. He'll get over it.'

'It's a wonder he didn't break his thigh.'

'He could have been killed,' Norman said with heat. 'We've got to stop him going up in the granary at night.'

'You've got a hope.' Rachel was scathing. 'It's the only place from where he can watch those owls. That's why he put the nest box just outside the granary window. You could fix a handrail though, darling; there's a stack of timber in the coach-house.'

'That's an idea. We've got to take care of him at his age.'

'He was demanding champagne with his breakfast,' Iris said.

They stared at her. 'Champagne!' Norman snorted. 'And he won't buy a pot of paint so I can do the windows! Anyone would think we were paupers. There's all those cottages bringing in thirty, forty quid a week, and the butcher's bill hasn't been paid for two months! Can't you get him organised to pay a few bills? Hell, Sandra paid in advance for the mill cottage: two months! That's over two hundred quid.'

'How did you know she paid in advance?' Rachel was askance, then vicious. 'Oh, *she* told you—'

'She talks too much.'

'She is—a trifle indiscreet.' She was childishly venomous, then her tone changed, became earnest: 'Grandad has to plough everything back into the estate, you know that. We've always lived on tick; you've no idea what it costs to keep up this place, and the land; why, you've only got to look at our roof, let alone Corn's buildings. And for God's sake, don't talk about money today; he's going to have enough excitement without that—and his blood pressure can't be normal at his age—can it, Iris?'

'He'll see a few more birthdays yet, providing he takes care of himself.'

'So when are you going to let him start on the champagne?' Norman asked drily.

'I'll stall him as long as possible but if it comes to a choice of evils and he's going to

12

work himself into a tantrum we could allow a small glass before lunch, but no more than that. And we'll need to watch him carefully once he gets up or he'll be sneaking down the cellar for a bottle if he can't get to the fridge.'

'We can soon stop that.' Norman took a huge key from a nail beside the cooker. In a corner of the flagged kitchen was a door which he locked. 'Where can we hide the key?'

'In the bread crock,' Rachel suggested. 'Can you handle him, Iris, if he finds the cellar's locked?'

'I'll manage; don't worry about it.'

'I don't know what we'd do without you.' Norman's eyes shone with sincerity.

'You're a tower of strength,' Rachel echoed, then she winced as if in pain. 'It's ghastly: living with old people.'

'He's no trouble.' Iris scoured a pan with capable hands.

'It's not that.' The girl's face was dismal with suffering. 'It's remembering he's so old, and some time soon he's got to—I mean: eighty-seven! I can't bear it at times; I feel I'm going to blow my top. I don't care about dying myself, it could be rather nice: beautiful—and sad?—but, for other people—' she stared at her husband with such intensity that he was embarrassed,

'—people you love. . . . God! I'd rather it was me!'

He put an arm round her shoulders. 'Darling!' He nuzzled her ear.

'Don't!' she gasped and flinched away from him to be overwhelmed immediately by contrition. 'I'm sorry, but you make it worse. We've got no *right* to be happy.'

He changed gear effortlessly. 'After seventy every day is a bonus. He's had seventeen years since seventy and he's happy as a sandboy—even now. He revelled in that fight with the nuclear power people, and he's enjoying his fall.'

Iris turned and stared at him.

'Oh yes,' he went on, 'he's not really paranoid, you know; he's just playing up to the image. He adores drama—like you, darling—' he regarded his wife with affectionate amusement but kept his tone light, '—don't you remember him telling us, when we thought there was going to be a public inquiry, that the Atomic Energy Authority would stop at nothing to get the site? Including murder, he said. Surely you haven't forgotten him ringing the chief constable to ask where he could get trained Alsatians for protection?'

Rachel giggled. 'And Pritchard telling him

he'd buy Dobermans to stop our Alsatians chasing his sheep!'

'He's a character,' Iris said fondly. 'He was swearing like a trooper at me this morning.'

'Back to normal,' Rachel commented with a hint of possessiveness. 'Did he upset you?'

'Not me, dear. I didn't like him working himself into a rage though, for his own sake. We've got to make allowances. He's a little selfish, like Norman says.'

'But not senile.' Rachel turned to her husband. 'He just likes scenes. I don't know how the party's going to go. I bet he's got something planned, something naughty. I mean, he *is* naughty, isn't he, darling?'

'We'll cope,' he said firmly. 'After all, we're all family. If we sense him building up to something, we can all gang up on him: a kind of flattening conspiracy.'

She looked at him darkly. 'Don't kid yourself. You've not known him as long as I have. He's got the telephone in his room; how do you know what he's planned? And anyway, we won't all be family at the party. Samuel's all right, but there's the new tenant at Captain's Cottage and she's not even what you'd call a close friend. He says he hasn't seen her for seven years.'

'She's all to the good then. He told me he'd

15

asked her to the party because it may be his last—typical!—and his last chance of talking about the Alps to someone who's climbed them, so what they'll do is get in a huddle in a corner and all we have to do is leave them to it, making sure there are no bottles in reach or he'll get plastered.'

'Suppose she's an alcoholic?' Iris put in.

'Oh Iris!' Rachel sparkled. 'She's frumpish and fat and she wears brown tweeds—'

'In this heat!' Norman was aghast.

'She'll wear a brown linen costume then, and she's a J.P. and she writes for magazines—women's weeklies, stuff like that.'

'Nothing to say she's not an alcoholic,' Iris persisted.

'A J.P.?' Norman grinned. 'You're quite a cynic. Seriously, she sounds just right for the old man. And then there's Samuel who'd be oil on any troubled waters, well: oily—hello, car coming.'

'It sounds like Mum.'

A big white Mercedes swept into the sunlit yard and stopped, punishing its springs. A woman with red hair that was a shade too red got out and came towards the windows carrying a package. 'Hello darlings,' she called. 'How is he?'

16

She didn't wait for an answer and a moment later her steps could be heard in the passage. She appeared in the doorway, a darkly tanned woman in a cream trouser suit. Round her thin throat and wrists gold chains and bangles clashed elegantly with her movements. She gave her daughter a perfunctory peck on the cheek.

'You look tired, sweetie; it's this heat. Why don't you two go down to the beach for a while? I'm sure Iris can manage on her own. How are you, Norman? How's Roderick?'

'Straining at the leash. Is that his present?'

'The tripod for his new binoculars—yes. Rupert wouldn't let me bring those; he said they'd fall off the seat, the way I drove. However. I'll put this with the rest of the stuff in the drawing room, then I'll go up.'

'You stay down here until we've got him dressed,' Rachel told her. 'He'd hate you to see him in bed. Coming, Norman?'

Doreen Bowen raised her eyebrows at their backs, then shrugged and turned to the housekeeper quietly assembling her equipment for baking.

'You've got a lot on your hands today, Iris. How's it going?'

'We're managing.'

17

'I can't imagine you doing anything else.'

'I wouldn't hold a job down long if I panicked when there was a bit of entertaining.'

'No. You're a good worker, I'll say that for you. Can't be much fun here all the same.' Doreen looked round the old-fashioned kitchen with disparagement. 'Getting paid regularly?'

'I'm paid.'

'It *is* my business.' The cool gaze was designed to leave the other in no doubt concerning her own position in the household. 'There's no money here, you know.'

'It's quiet.' Iris was phlegmatic. 'The hotel was too much for me.'

'So you said. The pay was good though.'

'We're both at the same time of life, Mrs Bowen; a hot hotel kitchen's not my cup of tea in the season. I'm not over-paid here, but I'm my own boss and I can cope with your father-in-law.'

'I'm sure you can. And he's grown fond of you.'

'That makes things run smoothly. No friction.'

'A cushy billet.'

'It's a comfortable position well enough.'

18

Doreen licked her lips. 'Well, you'll be keeping a close eye on him today; he can't take much more excitement after the campaign. And his accident.'

Iris opened the oven door and tested the temperature with her hand. 'He's still saying he was pushed.'

'Everyone goes a little odd with age. Even middle age—with some. I hope you don't mind my mentioning it, dear, but you've split a seam: under the arm. No, the left one.'

'I'm putting on weight,' Iris said ruefully.

'You could do with a new dress, but I don't suppose it matters, in the kitchen.'

'Cooks don't have much call to bother about their appearance.'

'Quite. Not terribly hygienic though, is it?' Doreen stared pointedly at a grease stain on the front of the brown dress. 'Perhaps I could find you some old thing of mine—if you could get into it.'

'Don't trouble, Mrs Bowen; I'm a bit particular about the feel of stuff. This dress is silk.'

'You could have fooled me.'

Doreen turned and sauntered out of the kitchen. Behind her the housekeeper switched on her transistor and measured flour into a pastry bowl. Her face was expressionless. Pop from Radio One filled the room while outside the wide windows the heat built up for another sweltering June day.

CHAPTER TWO

DOWN IN THE village, in Captain's Cottage, Melinda Pink, J.P., was starting to unpack on the first day of her holiday, if one discounted the travelling time. The journey from Cornwall to West Wales cannot be done comfortably in one day, and she had spent the night in Welshpool, breakfasting in her room on coffee and Health Food biscuits, and pushing on early this morning as the river mists started to dissolve in the sun.

Before nine o'clock, and still ahead of the tourist traffic, she'd stopped on the last pass for the view. Ahead and below, the bulk of Wales fined down to a long arm flung out in the Celtic Sea. On its southerly coast there were sandy bays and small resorts, the bays diminishing in size and number towards the west, and each demarcated by peninsulas with headlands, and islands in the sea.

Inland a pattern of fields was broken by isolated groups of spiky hills. Even at this hour the land was hazy and had the animate yet sluggish air of an animal drowsing away the morning with the knowledge that activity would be pointless, blasted by the heat.

So Miss Pink thought, drinking coffee from her vacuum flask with all the windows open and the jacket of her safari suit sticking to her back. Blissfully she looked forward to the week's rest: idling along the cliffs and watching birds where the closest she would come to stress would be vicarious fear at sight of a patrolling predator. A car passed in a stench of fumes. It was time to move on.

She ran down through a village set on a shelf below the pass where the tar was already softening, and then she was among the patterned fields, and drystone walls gave way to high banks which appeared to be of earth, but where the soil had eroded, the basic structure was revealed in uniform rows of rounded stones. The tops of the banks were covered with wild flowers: pink and white and blue and lemon. No one had sprayed poison, no Council lengthman had been here with his sickle. There was a scent of honeysuckle and baking earth.

The haze increased and out of it loomed the summits of Riffli's range. She passed the last of the inland villages and now there were only scattered farmsteads bare and bright in a treeless landscape where, exposed to winter gales, nothing grew higher than the hawthorns, and they were distorted, their branches brown with faded blossom and all strained towards the east.

Her junction was marked by a shabby signpost. ABERSAINT, it said in scarcely legible print. No mileage was given; that was irrelevant. The lane dipped to a combe under the flank of the stony hills and there was nothing beyond Abersaint but the sea. The water was a molten expanse at the mouth of the valley, but the shore was hidden by woods which climbed the combe like a stippled pelt. On her right, through gateways to fields the size of paddocks and overgrown by bracken, she caught glimpses of a river glinting in its rocky bed.

The combe narrowed to a ravine and the lane dived into a tunnel formed by massive sycamores. The aspect was south and the woods sheltered by the hills. Birdsong was loud in the chequered depths.

She passed no house after she left the main road and, but for the rickety gates, she might have been in the wilderness. Even the lane had an air of mystery, its surface evidence of man's passing but scarcely of his existence. And then, suddenly, the trees stopped and she emerged to a dazzle of sunlight and civilisation.

The heart of Abersaint was a few cottages

grouped on two sides of a square green which was suffering from the drought. On the left, set back a little, was a store which doubled as the Post Office. It was long and whitewashed under a slate roof. The door was open and on a rack outside was a collection of paperback books while the walls were hung with nets of coloured balls, columns of postcards and guidebooks, and a sheaf of plastic kites.

Beyond the Post Office was a terraced row of single-storey cottages, their trim painted in varying pastel shades, their chimneys substantial but squat, and fronted by brilliant patches of gardens. Their windows were open, swimsuits and towels drying on the sills. These would be holiday cottages. Beyond them, in the far corner of the green, was a long house with three dormer windows and behind it a belfry showed at the end of a roof: the kind of belfry that is merely an open structure to hold the bell. Dark tombstones stood stark against the sea.

Miss Pink stopped below the Post Office to get her bearings. She had come here once, many years ago, on a wet autumnal day with a gale so strong as to preclude bird-watching from high cliffs. She had returned up the combe to walk inland where it was safe. Now she looked round benignly, relishing an atmosphere reminiscent of childhood holidays.

There was a fine double-arched bridge with the river a brawling stream above it but below broadening to a tidal basin where a number of boats, from dinghies to small yachts, were mirrored on a sheet like glass. Every mast supported a statuesque gull and, for a moment, nothing moved except the traveller stepping from her car and smoothing creases on her powerful thighs. Then a dark plump woman appeared at the door of the Post Office and approached, smiling diffidently.

'Would you be Miss Pink, the lady that's taken Captain's Cottage? I'm Mrs Hughes, the postmistress. The key's at the hotel. That's the big place across the water.'

Miss Pink thanked her and commented on the lovely weather.

'Hot,' Mrs Hughes qualified, 'I'm glad to get out from them freezers. We need air-conditioning in that shop.' She laughed, treating it as a joke, and for a few moments they exchanged platitudes on the need for rain and the problems of gardeners, while each assessed the other with the steady regard of ladies hailing from different villages. An inquisitive but basically good-natured body, Miss Pink thought as she returned to her car

25

and drove across the bridge and along the quay to a tall white building on the edge of the strand.

An angular receptionist with green eye shadow told her that Mr Bowen would be down with the key. She went back to her office and could be heard telephoning.

Miss Pink peeped through doorways, discovering a comfortable bar and a television lounge, their windows fronting on the quay. There was thick carpeting, soft armchairs, heavy polished tables and bowls of flowers. She was admiring a framed chart in the hall when a man came down the stairs and introduced himself as Rupert Bowen.

He was a stout fellow with a large nose but although he carried too much weight he looked as if he lived out of doors a good deal. His thinning hair was auburn against a brick-red skull, the forehead and fleshy cheeks roughened by exposure to the weather. He resembled a genial bloodhound and when he moved to the door with her she noted that he had the easy grace possessed by some stout men.

He apologised for the absence of his wife who had gone to Riffli to pay her respects to old Roderick on his birthday. He would go up himself when Doreen returned to the hotel.

'In that case,' Miss Pink remarked, 'I'll postpone my own appearance until this evening. He won't want a lot of excitement before his party.'

'What my father wants and what he should have are at opposite poles.' Rupert gave a throaty chuckle. 'Here he's been running the campaign against the Atomic Energy people for months. . . . You know about that?'

'I followed it carefully.'

'Wrote to your M.P., I hope?'

'My own, and yours, and, of course, the Minister. I've an official standing too, as a director of Plas Mawr Adventure Centre.'

'Of course. Prevailing winds and all that, what? Radioactive particles wafting over Snowdonia. Strontium 90 in the kids' joints? We've all become experts on pollution since the campaign. I was saying: he organised that, and now he's had this fall—'

'I didn't know. Was he hurt?'

'Colours like a mackerel all down one side, but nothing broken, fortunately. Fell down the granary steps three nights ago.'

'I *am* sorry. Does that mean the party's postponed?'

'He won't hear of it. I suggested last night that we have a buffet in his room and he blew up! Called me a namby-pamby! "Right," I

27

said, "We'll eat downstairs as arranged—"
and left it hanging, implying, you know, that
he should make a brief appearance. He said
quietly—and if you know the old man, he's
never quiet unless he's cooking something
up—said in a rather pathetic tone that "that
would be very nice". He's as cunning as a
weasel.'

'I have sat on committees with him,' she
said meaningly.

'I know; that would be when you lived in
Snowdonia. He gets worse with age. How do
you like Cornwall?'

'Pleasant, but too far from the hills.'

'Ah, you climbers are all the same. Doing
any climbing here?'

'Not on the sea cliffs,' she assured him
firmly.

'Thank God. They're unclimbable. I take
the guests in close to the Head to see the birds.
It's a frightening spot. Engine packed in once
underneath them; calm sea and a full tide
luckily, but when I'd got her going again and
we were pottering along below, I took a closer
look at them and reckoned that if we'd had to
go ashore there wasn't anywhere that we
could have scaled them. Terrible place for a
shipwreck. You'll have to come out with us
some time.'

'That would be delightful.' Her tone was lukewarm.

'Oh, I've got a new engine now. Can't take risks with the guests, you know.'

They smiled. The receptionist appeared in the doorway. 'Telephone, Mr Bowen.'

'I mustn't keep you,' Miss Pink said.

'That's all right. Look, there's your cottage.' He pointed. 'Across the river beyond the church. We've stocked the fridge and if there's anything you need, let us know. You're having your main meal here, except tonight, aren't you? This is the front door key. The back door opens on the terrace and the key for that's in the lock. There's a note about switches and things on the wall beside the fridge. The immersion heater's on for a bath.'

'Really,' Miss Pink beamed, 'You've been most accommodating.'

'No trouble, dear lady, none at all.'

'And when you go to Riffli, please give your father my regards and tell him I'm looking forward to this evening.'

She drove back along the quay, nosed through the square where, on the seaward side, the tar was drifted with sand, and turning through the gap, stopped outside a gate bearing a neat board: 'Captain's Cottage'. Crimson fuchsia hung over the wall and

29

through the gate there was a glimpse of a roof on a lower level. The lane was narrow and she remembered tardily that Rupert Bowen had forgotten to tell her where to leave the car.

She walked down the length of the garden wall. It abutted against the gable-end of the long cottage facing up the green. On the other side of the lane were two modern garages with up-and-over doors, both of which were closed. She was pondering these when a voice said: 'Can I help you?'

A thickset man who could be in his mid-forties was smiling from the doorway of the long house. He wore neat blue jeans and a navy shirt.

'You must be Miss Pink. I'm Samuel Honey. The top one's your garage. The key's in the house. Let me help you unload the car.'

He insisted on seeing her into the cottage, talking all the time, delighted to be of assistance. He took her bags to the best bedroom which fronted on the sea; the other, he pointed out, looked over the graveyard. He opened the fridge to reveal a crammed interior, showed her the immersion heater switch, the window that stuck and how to ease it open, and lastly, unlocked the kitchen door and displayed the terrace: flagged, with an iron table and chairs, and another fuchsia hedge that ensured privacy from people on the sand twenty feet below. In the corner was a small gate: her personal way to the beach. There was a second at the bottom of the steps which was kept padlocked. She asked him to stay for a cup of tea.

They sat on the terrace drinking Lapsang Souchong and he told her that the house had been built in the eighteenth century by a sea captain who had made his fortune in the slave trade. Honey, himself, had lived next door for five years after being invalided out of the R.A.F. 'Spinal compression,' he explained: 'Ejection seats—whoomph!'

'Welsh winters must be quite a trial. Backs are always happier in a dry climate.'

'Ah, Malta!' He sighed. 'But the cost of living. . . . And Roderick's so feudal: strips the visitors for all they're worth, and charges his friends a peppercorn rent. And I've got ties here. . . . .' A curious expression creased his eyes, passed, and he stretched his legs extravagantly. 'I understand you're joining us for the party tonight. You'll enjoy it.' He realised she had caught a note of doubt in this and he qualified it: 'We—that is, the company are a mixed bag. I don't know if you've met the family?'

'I saw Rupert when I went over for the

31

key.'

'Ah yes. Rupert. He's married to Doreen. Rachel's mother.'

His mind was far from what he was saying. Miss Pink's bland gaze wandered to the fuchsia hedge which, she thought absently, would be the better for pruning. Judging by the sounds of activity the beach was filling up, but the noise of people was unobtrusive. The heat lay over the bay like a blanket, and children's cries, lacing the whisper of gentle waves, had a somnolent quality, like the calls of sleepy gulls.

The village stood in the corner of the bay, and beyond the hotel the peninsula jutted into the sea, densely wooded on this side but, with the sun full on the glistening foliage, she could just make out a tall chimney and a gleam of roof where Riffli stood a hundred feet above the shore. At this point there were no cliffs; they lay beyond the woods, round the corner, fronting the sea.

She moved restlessly. The tea was hot and the air on the terrace close against the white wall was stifling. He put down his cup.

'You'll be wanting to get yourself straight. Come down to my place at six and we'll walk to Riffli together; no sense in taking a car, and we don't want to. Roderick never stints the wine on birthdays. Is that all right with you?'

She acquiesced and showed him out, then she changed into thin worn jeans and, with a small rucksack on her back and binoculars slung round her neck, she set out for the cliffs: the picture of an elderly spinster happily intent on a strenuous and innocent day's bird-watching.

CHAPTER THREE

THE CLIFFS WERE convex. The mass of the peninsula was an elevated plateau of farmland, pasture and arable, but towards Riffli Head the boundary bank (topped by fencing) stopped short before a heath of gorse and heather. Then came a stretch of turf and the first drop: of grass which fell away for one or even two hundred feet in dangerously steep slopes contoured by pale threads of sheep paths. The sea showed at the bottom of the grass, but the eye of the climber could calculate the vertical distance between grass and sea if only from the scale of the low-flying cormorants which were black specks identified by flight alone.

Then in places, from a sideways slant, the structure of the coast was revealed with the gaunt cliffs plunging to the sea under the long brown slopes. Anyone slipping from a sheep path would have no chance, only time to think—slithering out of control down nothing more than scorched grass—of that moment when the grass would end and the vertical rock begin.

Miss Pink, treading a sheep path warily,

stopped at a knob of rock and, looking back, started to take deep breaths to combat a rising panic. But the plummeting cliff she'd traversed above was striated by ledges and white with droppings and when she'd sat down and steadied the binoculars on her knees, she had in view rank upon rank of nesting guillemots. She watched until her eyes were tired and then looked out to sea where the tide-race slipped through the channel between the headland and the twin islands of Saint Pedrog. These were low but rocky, their crests crowned with rank vegetation. Through the glasses she could see the puffins standing outside their burrows.

She gave a sigh of pleasure and leaned back against the slope. She was at the side of a great gully or funnel which had the effect of increasing the angle, but even here a sheep path ran into the back and out again. Looking up, she saw black scree and a blacker hole, and recalled that there were old manganese mines in the district. On the skyline was a stretch of new fencing and a stile.

The sides of the funnel ran down in raised spines to the top of the cliffs, that on the far side continuing in an overhanging buttress but on the facet towards her was a magnificent slab over a hundred feet high. She looked down her own side of the funnel. Could there be a buttress here too? She started to descend, moving carefully from anthill to anthill, from rock to rock.

There was no sharp demarcation between grass and cliff, only the grass was more withered and there were arid patches of earth round rabbit holes; then bedrock appeared in a tilted pavement which steepened, but there were fissures in corners, and big cushions of thrift pink with blooms. Eventually her descent was blocked by a crack which was quite easy for as far as she could see but which appeared to be bottomless. Nothing was visible but the water perhaps a hundred feet below. A kittiwake floated out from underneath. She was above a massive overhang.

She glanced to her right and there at sea level, in the back of the cove and directly under the funnel, gaped an enormous cavern. Against the gloom of its mouth the kittiwakes drifted in the sunshine. Young shag swam in the navy water which was very deep under the jut of the roof. The tide was ebbing with a few hours to go before the turn but although the water was clear, she couldn't see the bottom. This place would never dry out.

There was a watery snort. In the middle of the cove a grey seal appeared, the lustrous

36

eyes already turned to her as it surfaced, causing her to speculate, and not for the first time, how they could know an object of interest existed before they came up, let alone its exact position.

She found a corner in the shade and ate her lunch. There wasn't a breath of breeze. Close at hand she could hear a pair of fulmars talking quietly and she felt like an eavesdropper. Even the shade was hot. After lunch, she thought, she would return to the top, to level ground, have a short nap, then potter along the heath . . . keeping an eye open for adders . . . swim . . . if she could find a beach where it was safe . . .

The scream wakened her: a crescendo of astonishment and fright. There was pain in her neck and ribs and her hands scraped the rock frantically. There was an effect of immediate darkness but a more spacious one of brilliance, like viewing a stage from the auditorium. Birds and a human figure floated in the air. Awe over-rode panic and there was a fraction of delighted time when she knew, without surprise, that death was beautiful.

Then the scream broke in the gabble of an angry gull and a raven honked unseen. She sat up, wincing and rubbing the places where the rock had dug in while she slept. The binoculars were round her neck; nothing had rolled off. She blinked across the water. The human figure was real; not floating but climbing down the great slab on the other side of the cove.

She didn't have to peer to be sure that there was no rope and no companion; the sun picked out every groove in the rock, every move of the climber, and these had the precise and dedicated absorption of one who fancied herself unobserved.

She wore a blue bikini and she was very brown. Her hair was a tawny mass. She was barefooted and sturdy and she moved, not like an animal for that place was impassable for anything without hands, but like a natural climber, which was where Miss Pink had got that momentary impression of floating. The silent descent had the fluid quality of water dropping down the rock.

The slab ran into barnacled shelves exposed by the tide and the climber turned and looked out to sea. The seal came up about a hundred yards from the shore and the girl lowered herself into the water and swam towards it with a lazy breast stroke. The beast trod water with waving flippers, watching her approach, then humped and dived. A low

38

chuckle rose to Miss Pink.

The girl curved back towards the buttress. There was no sign of the raven and the gulls had settled again. Kittiwakes sped in and out of the cavern.

Then from high above, confusingly high when the attention had been directed downwards for some time, there was a kind of commotion, a clattering and thumping approaching fast, curiously familiar: an imprint in the convulsions of the brain which had recorded it decades ago, in the Alps, in a couloir. A rockfall.

Miss Pink gaped at the lip of the cliff above the cavern, glimpsed a figure on the skyline and then, out from the lip leapt a mass, a huge jagged disc turning in the sunlight. It fell with a rush of air past the cavern and crashed into the water like a bomb. The impact reverberated against rock walls, spray rose and splattered, and the birds erupted in a cacophony of panic.

She glanced seaward. The girl was staring up at the cliffs. Then she swam to the foot of the buttress, climbed out and started to make her way up the slab. Miss Pink didn't stay to watch. She was cramming her things in her rucksack in a state of furious shock.

As she emerged on the tilted pavement and

started to scramble up the grass she saw a man watching her from the scree tip outside the manganese mine. She didn't stop to think but somewhere in the back of her mind was the sensation of a terrier shaking a rat. When she reached the tip, he'd vanished, nor could she see him when she came out on level ground. She sat down, trembling from the exertion of rushing up the slope, and closed her eyes.

'You've hurt your hand.'

The girl in the blue bikini stood on the turf, her eyes searching the gorse. Miss Pink saw that the back of her own hand was smeared with blood.

'He was too quick for me,' she said. 'He got away.'

'He wouldn't do it if he wasn't such a good runner.' The tone was dry.

'You know him?' Miss Pink asked in astonishment.

'Our local hoodlum—although that's not fair. He's got problems.'

'We all have.' She didn't trouble to restrain her anger. 'You're not making excuses for a man who might have killed you?'

'*Me?* He didn't even know I was there. It was you he was after.'

Miss Pink was speechless.

'Oh, he didn't mean any harm,' the girl assured her earnestly. 'He was just trying to frighten you. It's his thing,' she explained as the other stared. 'He's always rolling rocks down on visitors. What he likes most is fellows with girls. They get on the sheep paths: chaps leading the girls by the hand—and Jakey drops a rock. The guys can't go after him because he's miles above, and because he can run fast, and anyway, by that time the girls are having hysterics. They're not happy on the paths to start with. Jakey's little game sends them over the edge. It'll happen literally one day.'

'But the man's a sadist!'

'Man? Didn't you see him? He's a boy. He's fourteen.'

Miss Pink asked weakly: 'Who is he?'

'Jakey Jones. His people work for us. I'm so sorry—' her manner became conventional, '—I should have introduced myself. I'm Roderick's grand-daughter: Rachel Kemp. And you're Miss Pink, I guess. I'm sorry that this should have happened. I'll have a talk with Jakey.'

Miss Pink said grimly: 'I think your grandfather would do more than that. How many birds does he injure with those rocks?'

'I know.' The girl looked anguished.

41

'That's why I don't tell Grandad, you see; he'd have a fit. You can't do anything with Jakey. If I'd seen any birds killed, I'd have felt like killing *him*, but there weren't any floating.' She thought about this. 'Yes,' she went on, 'I would have thumped him; he's got it coming. He should be at school right now but, of course, he's playing truant.'

'And his parents?' There was a trace of resignation in Miss Pink's voice and the girl caught it and nodded. She shrugged muscular shoulders. Wet curls shaded her eyes and left the sharp blade of her nose too prominent.

'Wait till you see them. There's no broken home but he's an only child and spoilt. His mother's a compulsive cleaner—you know the type: all bleach and Jeyes' fluid, and wall-to-wall plastic in the parlour to protect the carpet. And Jakey can do nothing wrong. He runs around with Ossie Hughes from the Post Office who's fat and not very bright but Thirza Jones says Ossie corrupts *Jakey*! Ossie would jump over the cliff if Jakey told him to.'

'And the father?'

'He's screwy. He used to work for Lord Barmouth. He was the handyman actually but he tells people he was the butler. Got a peculiar veneration for "the Lord": the Lord would never use a knife for the Stilton, or put milk in tea first—it's weird, honestly. We think he's funny but he must be hell to live with particularly for a boy with no sense of humour, or one that's twisted—like Jakey's.'

'What's the father's attitude to his son's hooliganism—such as terrifying visitors by starting rockfalls?'

'He blocks out the facts, let alone the rumours. Some parents can do that. If someone said they saw Jakey throwing stones at sheep or shop-lifting then his father would swear they were mistaken. He's never been caught, you see, except by my husband. He gave Jakey a hell of a thrashing when he found him breaking up Grandad's nest boxes. Two nights later we had all the tyres slashed on our Mini. No proof, of course, but Norman says he'll get Jakey for it one day.'

Miss Pink exhaled heavily.

'It was a shame you had to run into him on your first walk,' Rachel said politely.

'How did he know I was there—and why are you so sure he didn't intend the rock for you?'

The girl stared at her intensely. 'I didn't know you were there,' she said obliquely, and stopped. She stood up. 'Come down to the tip: where he was standing.'

They went down to the scree at the mouth

43

of the old mine. The tip itself was very un-
stable; there were more large rocks lying
about and below, in the funnel, they saw the
marks gouged in the soil by the falling
boulder.

'You see,' Rachel pointed out, 'the cove is
invisible from here but he could have seen you
on that buttress. I never saw you till after the
rock fell.' Her tone was accusing. 'How long
had you been there?'

'I saw you go down the slab.'

'Did you?' Again that brooding stare.

'Does Jakey know that there's a way down
and that you swim there?'

'No one knows.'

Miss Pink felt a little uncomfortable. 'If
you'd rather I didn't publicise it, you'd better
explain. Your family would disapprove, of
course.'

'Can I trust you?'

'Well, you climb very competently: within
your limit; I see no danger there, but I can
quite believe your people would be horrified—except—' she smiled, '—your grandfather. Does your husband climb? I know
your father doesn't.'

'Norman doesn't climb.' For a long
moment the girl stared down the funnel. 'This
is my place,' she said eventually, 'my very

own—and now *you* know.' She sounded stricken.

'I can hold my tongue.' Miss Pink was tart. 'But Jakey's the danger. Suppose he were to drop a rock on a person crossing this slope and you were swimming in the mouth of the cavern right where the other rock fell? It doesn't bear thinking about.'

'I couldn't swim there. When Pritchard, our tenant, put up that new fence, he rolled all the old wire and posts down the funnel and the water is full of barbed wire now. You can see it with a very low tide. Grandad was livid because of the seals.'

'Do they breed there?'

'No, fortunately. There's no breach and no ledges in the cavern. It only goes a short distance and the walls are sheer inside. The birds nest high up in the roof. So there's nothing interesting inside. I always swim way out beyond the wire. It's quite safe, I promise you. I only do it when it's flat calm. Daddy doesn't know, nor Norman, no one—except you. *Please!*'

Miss Pink shrugged. 'I don't see how it can do any harm providing you do take care. Everyone needs a private place. No, I won't talk. Who taught you to climb?'

'People who stayed here. We used to come

45

down for holidays before my parents took over the pub and there were often climbers staying at Riffli in the summer. Grandad likes people. They took me climbing in the mountains but I like it best on my own. No ropes, you see.'

'And have you explored these old mines?'

'They're not worth it. They're either too easy like this level—' they turned and regarded the mouth of the tunnel, '—it only goes back for forty feet or so and there's nothing but sheeps' bones. They come here to die. Otherwise, they're too difficult, like the lower level.'

'There's a level lower down? I didn't see it.'

'Just a shaft—but hairy. Come and see; there are some nice plants.'

They descended by well-graded zig-zags outside the funnel: the way the old miners had made. At the foot of the grass slope and at the top of the cliffs the path came in to the funnel to debouch on a wide ledge on the edge of nothing. As far as this the track was safe-guarded by a raised bank on its outer edge but the terminal platform had no protection of any kind. Far below the sea was silent under the shadowed buttress.

At the back of the platform was a gaping hole about ten feet wide. Its sides were damp

46

and festooned with small ferns.

'Here's some red broomrape,' Rachel said proudly, and Miss Pink turned away from the shaft.

'*Orobanche alba*,' she breathed. 'Can it be? Yes, here's thyme. It's a parasite on thyme. Would you believe it!'

'That's nice; I hadn't realised it was rare.'

They poked about a bit but, finding nothing so good as the *orobanche*, they turned back to the ferns in the shaft.

'How deep is this?' Miss Pink dropped a small stone delicately. There was no sound of its landing.

'Could be more dead sheep down there,' Rachel observed. 'No one ever troubled to plug these holes. The land's private property and there's no public footpath. Grandad's attitude is that if anyone's simple enough to venture on these cliffs and get into trouble, society's well rid of them. 'Least, that's what he *says*.'

'Bark's worse than his bite.' Miss Pink looked at her watch. 'I must be getting back; I'm in need of a bath before the party.'

'If you run into Jakey, take a firm line.'

'I'll certainly do that. Do you suppose he knows who I am?'

'A J.P.? That's very likely. Fancy him

47

daring to go that far! I should think you're very firm with delinquents though. You wouldn't be frightened of him, would you?'

'Not of him, but of the damage he can do.'

'You're so right. He's clever and cruel. He finds people's weak points—I mean, like you watching birds, and then he can hit you where it hurts most. Sam's terrified of him—that's a guy in the village. He's got a kitten. He won't let it out of the front door because it might stray and then Jakey could find it. He locks it in when he goes away.'

'Good gracious! For how long?'

'I mean, just when he's away for a few hours. He's got a friend—' the tone hardened, '—in the woods. A visiting . . . A kind of visitor. Not something we like to publicise actually.' She was trying to sound adult and patronising but her voice cracked. 'A—' She hesitated. Miss Pink's brows rose. The girl's eyes were wide and her mouth twisted.

'She's a bloody whore!'

CHAPTER FOUR

A SWEET CHILD, but unruly.' Samuel reversed the mincer and extracted a piece of bone. 'Her grandfather calls her a tomboy. Curious word. What was she doing?' Miss Pink had given him to understand that she'd met Rachel in the fields.

'Looking at flowers.'

'Yes?' His kitten, sitting to attention on the fridge, parted tiny jaws in mute admonishment to him to get on with the job of preparing supper. 'Manners,' Samuel said absently and turned to Miss Pink. 'Were you able to help her?'

'I knew a few things that she didn't, but she's quite knowledgeable; self-taught, I suppose. Not always a good thing; mistakes get perpetuated.'

'How's that?'

'There's no one more experienced to push you into the right channels.'

He ran his tongue over his lips, his concentration riveted on mixing a spoonful of chicken with a few shreds of carrot.

'What's the trouble?' Miss Pink asked brutally.

49

He threw her a furtive look. 'Well— nineteen, you know; still virtually adolescent, isn't it? And just married?' His voice rose with each question as if he were testing it out on her. He tried another tack: 'And the campaign against the nuclear power people—' he was rallying, '—Lord! That would send anyone round the bend! The ultimate, isn't it? Have you read *On the Beach*—the atomic cloud approaching New Zealand? I'll lend it to you. Caithness! Supper—and don't gobble. He's sick when he gobbles. Come and have a sherry. I do love that caftan, dear; you look like one of those splendid ladies in a Somerset Maugham story.'

He ushered her into his living room: a large light place extending the depth of the house, with wicker furniture and sisal matting, and Van Gogh's 'Ravine' on an ivory wall. She watched his face as he poured the drinks. He was less ingenuous than he appeared. He was quite glamorous this evening, in a crisp parody of khaki drill with a cravat in printed silk: a smart outfit curiously at variance with the bluff face and innocent eyes. Innocent? How could they be with that furtive manner? It was obvious that he was dissimulating.

'There was a boy rolling stones down the cliffs,' she said, and for a moment those eyes were vulnerable before they emptied of expression and she was reminded of a reptile house and other eyes: behind strike-proof glass.

'The idea is to frighten trippers to death.'

'Since no one else was there,' she lied, 'he was trying to get me.'

'Really.' He exhaled slowly. 'How far will he go? Did you catch him?'

'No. I told Rachel about it. She didn't seem all that surprised.' She was interested to see that mention of Rachel in this context didn't disturb him.

'We all know Jakey's rolling-stone trick.' He was preoccupied but not wary. 'All except Roderick. He's too old to know . . . That's what Rachel maintains, and Doreen. But someone has to come up with a way of dealing with Jakey Jones. He's a monster in his own way.'

'It's disturbing. Is there no one who has any influence with him?'

'Oddly enough, Rachel has. She's not afraid of him, and he's got some kind of respect for her. He's scared of heights for one thing; he'll never go on the cliffs, always stays at the top to drop his rocks, but Rachel trots all over those ghastly slopes; I've seen her.'

'On the cliffs?'

51

'Oh no! On the grass slopes—but they're just as dangerous. I don't like it.' He glanced at his watch. 'Time we were moving.'

Miss Pink put down her half-finished drink and picked up her handbag. He locked the cottage and they set out across the green carrying their presents. Hers was a picture of the Weisshorn, his a new pair of climbing breeches, he'd confided, copied from a pair taken from the old man's wardrobe.

Seated on the parapet of the bridge, two boys watched their approach, the one with fine, almost feminine features, the other plump and bovine, but the expressions of both blank and disturbing. Samuel said 'Good evening, Ossie,' but neither lad responded.

Instead of turning left along the fish quay, they kept straight ahead, up the slope on a dusty track which climbed and then curved to contour the hill towards Riffli's woods. They passed through a gate beside a cattle grid and Miss Pink, glancing back, saw that the two figures still sat immobile on the bridge, their faces turned to the hill. Samuel, too, looked back.

'Is that Jakey Jones?'

'Yes.'

His hand trembled as he latched the gate. Miss Pink was well aware that violence bred violence, also that sometimes the current might be short-circuited. 'Tell me something about the people I'm going to meet,' she demanded as they turned to the track.

He blinked and frowned, surfacing from some strange depths. 'You know Roderick, and you've met Rachel. Rupert, her father, is just what he seems: no dark waters there; he enjoys playing mine host, particularly in the season when the pub's crowded. He's gregarious, not over-fond of hard work—demanding work, that is. He was some kind of oil executive but it wasn't his scene. His wife's a good business woman, a little—flamboyant—' he glanced at her, '—rather prickly, the kind of person who's good with the help but doesn't get on all that well with other ladies—nearer her own station.' His tone implied that she wasn't meant to take this as a joke. 'Of course, Rupert's a charmer,' he added as if in extenuation. 'Then there's Norman Kemp. Twenty-five . . .' His eyes moved from the woods to the sea. 'Attractive.' There was a further pause then, smoothly: 'Thick pale hair, reckless eyes set rather far apart, a long thin mouth, hard body; mad on power boats—' his voice dropped, '—but no boat. Rachel only married him three months ago. Brought him home after the honeymoon

53

and they've been at Riffli ever since.'

'What's his background?'

He regarded her steadily. 'He was managing a hotel in Scotland. They met when she was ski-ing at Aviemore and they were married within weeks. Rachel's impulsive.' The words hung in the air.

'He must have ability,' Miss Pink said, 'to be a manager at twenty-five.'

'Yes,'—flatly.

'And what does he do here?'

'He—looks after things. I don't know if you're aware of it, but Rachel will come into the land, and the big house, when Roderick dies. It's an open secret.' He saw her surprise. 'You see, her father's not interested in the land. He's found his niche at the pub. Roderick owns that too and it must be worth a bomb. Not nearly so much as the land and all the cottages, of course, but none of that can be realised. Rupert will inherit the hotel but all Rachel will get is liabilities. The rents don't cover the outgoings. I warn you: don't let Roderick get on to taxes!'

'How much land is there?'

'Upwards of two thousand acres. Probably worth a hundred thousand or so.'

'Some people sell part to keep the bulk going,' she murmured.

'Not Roderick! He says the peninsula and the mountain—this high ground above us with the fort on top—have been one unit since his people came here and it's going to stay that way. Did you know he traces his ancestry back to prehistoric times?' He giggled. 'But he's got the features, you know: that long head and the prominent brow ridges and the big jaw. It's in Rupert and Rachel too, less in Rupert.'

'Ownership of land can excite intense passion.'

He glanced at her sharply, saw that this was not ridicule and burst out: 'The worst of it was: compulsory purchase!'

'What! Oh, you mean when the site was required for a nuclear power station. They could have forced him to sell.'

'Exactly. No one dared to mention it except the Press. He told them that the site would be acquired over his dead body—and Rachel's.'

'What was her feeling about that?'

'The same. To Rachel the Corn cromlech and the fort on Carn Goch are *family*. She and Roderick talk about the Old People as if they were next-door neighbours. It makes my scalp creep on a moonlit night when I walk home down this track.' They had come to the woods. A baby rabbit ran a few paces and

55

froze, sunlight in the shell-pink ears. 'She said nothing to you on these lines?' he pressed.

'We were more concerned with flora and fauna.'

There was silence for a while. The rabbit nipped into the undergrowth, the dust was soft under their feet. 'Are you interested in wildlife, Mr Honey?' she asked politely.

'Samuel, please. Not the really wild life, dear; the kind you have to perch on the edge of a precipice to observe. I like to look at the birds but from a nice safe boat. I had my fill of thrills in the Air Force. I trot out to the headland occasionally but I approach it through the fields. Those grass slopes above the cliffs petrify me! If I see a sheep down there, I can't bear to look, even though I'm on level ground at the top. All that space! And the wheeling birds! It gives me vertigo. This is *my* idea of Nature—' he waved an arm at the trees and the white scuts twinkling through the bluebell leaves. 'Baby rabbits: charming.'

Masonry showed ahead and the open space of a yard, but he drew her aside and along a path under huge rhododendrons where the sun failed to penetrate. They emerged on a lawn strewn with daisies, and above them rose the façade of the house.

It was built of local stone and was tall,

appearing taller by virtue of its towering chimneys set at either end of the high roof. In places slates had slipped and now projected beyond the gutters. The windows were large, many-paned, and of a later date than the house which was probably sixteenth century. The woodwork would have been the better for a coat of paint, but the shabbiness was endearing. The arch of the main doorway was of moulded stone and the door was oak. It stood ajar.

They stepped into a panelled hall and heard distant sounds of activity: music, the clatter of dishes, a burst of laughter. Glancing at a doorway on the left, Samuel called: 'Are you in there, Roderick?'

Miss Pink heard a familiar voice shout to them to come in. She entered the drawing room and was shocked to find her diminutive host, even smaller than she remembered him, engaged in a painful struggle to rise from a sofa. Hurrying forward, she took his hand, her greetings lost in his protests.

'I can stand up! They haven't finished me off yet!' But he sank back and glared at her. 'Never greeted a lady before stuck on me rump! By jove, but you're a fine figure of a woman, Melinda, and that gown does yer justice.' He leered at her. 'Still single? Not

57

married that lawyer feller, Roberts? Watcher doing standing there, Sam? Get me guest a drink.'

'Miss Pink!' Rachel hurried in, wearing floating blue chiffon which looked incongruous on her sturdy frame. 'How lovely to see you. Drinks, Grandad?'

'Time it came,' he growled. 'I'm gasping. Dammit, it's me birthday! Know what they did, Mel? Locked the cellar door!'

'You weren't supposed to move from this room,' Rachel protested. 'How did you know the cellar door was locked?'

'It's me own cellar, isn't it?'

Samuel patted her bottom and pushed her out of the room. Suddenly he looked very happy. 'We'll bring the booze,' he assured them, and followed. Miss Pink repeated her congratulations to her host.

'Thank you, my dear.' His voice sank. 'You see me risen from me death bed.'

'Don't try to fool me, Roderick. You've had far worse falls in your time. How far was it?'

'They've told you. Fifteen feet.' He leaned towards her and whispered: 'I was pushed!'

She regarded him expectantly but without concern.

'Not to say pushed,' he amended. 'Have they told you exactly what happened? No.

58

They won't have it. I'll tell you. I was watching a pair of tawnies in the dusk. Nest box outside the granary window. Been watching every night since the young hatched. Everyone knew about me owls. Got too dark to see any more, came out, took a step and trod on a bloody great branch! Off I went; if I hadn't gone sideways and down the steps, I'd have gone straight over the edge and landed on a pile of rocks. It would have meant a broken thigh at best. Done deliberately, Melinda; that branch was *put* there. There was no wind.'

'Is there a tree near?'

He shrugged.

'Was the branch rotten?'

'A *big* one, Melinda. I'd have heard it come down. They're saying me hearing's not what it was. Dammit, a great branch like that! Why, I can hear the howlets cheeping in the nest box.'

Miss Pink was silent.

'It's right up your street.' The faded eyes gleamed slyly at her. 'Any ideas?'

There were only two things she could think of to say.

'Have you any enemies?'

'Dozens.' He grinned fiercely.

'Who stands to gain?'

59

He was pulled up short. There was a swift moment of astonishment then—blankness, followed by simulated greed. 'What yer brought for me, eh?'

It was a credible imitation of senility. She glanced round the room where presents were stacked on flat surfaces. She rose and leaned her parcel against the panelling.

'You have to wait to open them all together.' She was deliberately maternal, paying him back. 'No cheating.'

They regarded each other carefully. She knew he was tempted to ask her to forget about the branch, to forget what he'd said, but there was a sound of people approaching and Samuel entered with champagne in a silver bucket. He was followed by a slim young man in a dark suit, cream shirt and a plain black tie.

Roderick was introducing Norman Kemp when Rachel returned. Behind her came a man with grizzled hair and sideboards, wearing evening dress. No one paid him any attention. Miss Pink listened to Norman Kemp enthusing about the weather.

Roderick had his eye on his presents. He caught her watching him and she knew he wasn't thinking about presents. Norman drew up a chair without interrupting the easy flow of his conversation. Rachel subsided on a pouffe, the chiffon settling like coloured feathers about her feet. The stranger in evening dress crossed the room bearing a loaded tray and presented it stiffly. His face was wooden. 'Thank you, Jones,' Roderick said. Rachel watched Miss Pink. Norman was explaining how to get on a surf board.

A woman in green and gold bustled into the room in a swirl of Chanel and tinkling bracelets. She was followed by Rupert Bowen.

'Good evening, Doreen.' Roderick made to rise but was restrained by his son's wife who stooped gracefully and laid her cheek to his. He looked uncomfortable.

The introductions over, the presents ceremony began, and Miss Pink moved so that they could be stacked on the sofa. The guests eddied, the attentive Jones circulated with the champagne, they drank Roderick's health. Outside, beyond the shadowed lawn, two Scots pines framed an expanse of blue water where a white sail was almost stationary. The stump of the far headland was hazy in the evening light.

Roderick opened Miss Pink's gift first and held it on his knees to stare at it. For a moment he was speechless and his eyes were moist. Samuel had to hang it at once, taking down the Eiger which hung between the windows.

'You've made the old gentleman very happy, madam.' It was smooth and respectful but carried an air of patronage. She met the bright eyes of Jones as he passed on his way to the sideboard.

A large woman in a white overall came to the door, glanced towards the sofa and retreated silently.

'Who was that?' Doreen asked. 'Iris?'

'A large woman in an overall.'

'Iris MacNally, the housekeeper.' Doreen took a step nearer. 'She used to cook for us at the hotel but she left after Easter; said she couldn't face the season. Of course, she's getting on.'

'I see. Have you managed to replace her?'

'Oh, we've got an excellent man now. Iris is a good cook but not quite at home in the kitchen. I imagine she thinks she should be a step higher on the ladder.' Doreen smiled thinly and adjusted a curl with a jangle of bracelets. 'With Jones pretending he's the butler, his wife livid at being treated as the scullery maid, and Iris thinking she's a cut above cooking, this kitchen must be like a zoo. Servants are a trial, aren't they?'

'I don't have them,' Miss Pink said pleasantly, 'I have an excellent house-keeper. We work as a team.'

'Really. Few people can afford them nowadays, of course, unless they're in Roderick's position.'

The present ceremony concluded, they crossed the hall to another panelled room, lit by wall-lights, with a refectory table and tall candles in branches silver sticks. Dinner was served by the deft and soft-footed Jones, obviously in his element and, observing his handling of the hock, Miss Pink found herself wondering what Jakey was up to at this moment.

Through the salmon and the delicious ducklings which followed, Roderick drew her out on the activities of her adventure centre, and on the travels of her friend and co-director, Ted Roberts, now in the Pyrenees. From there they proceeded, metaphorically speaking, to the Alps: the Eiger, the Weisshorn, the Matterhorn, and all the time she knew that the old man's heart wasn't in this talk of snow and ice but much nearer home. She was unhappy. He really was worried about that branch on the granary steps. Her eyes followed Jones. Could his son be that bad?

On their return to the drawing room Roderick sent for the kitchen staff. Rachel looked meaningly at Miss Pink. Mrs Jones was a tall bony person with haunted eyes who was obviously embarrassed by the company. On the other hand, Iris MacNally held herself with assurance as they drank their employer's health. She had removed her overall and now, in a tight black frock, one could guess that not so long ago she would have had a good body; the kind of brawny, broad-hipped form that Fuseli drew. Her hair had been set for the occasion, her eyebrows were finely plucked and her mouth was a bright slash of lipstick. Black lace was strained over massive shoulders; it was a cocktail dress: a little worn, like the wearer. There was an air of the fading slattern about her, but one who knew her place.

Jones was offering Roderick three packages on a salver. There was a bird book, a pen-and-pencil set, and a five-year diary. This last was from Iris and the thought behind it touched him deeply. Miss Pink saw Doreen's lip curl.

When the women had gone back to the kitchen there was a feeling of anti-climax, as if the evening was running down. Roderick started to fidget and people took it in turns to sit beside him and try to keep him amused. Miss Pink was talking flowers to Rachel when her eye caught a movement in the hall. A tall slim girl in a red dress came into the room and for a moment no one else noticed her.

She had large, slightly protruberant blue eyes, high cheek bones and a tanned translucent skin. Her hair was jet-black with a heavy fringe, its hard gloss contrasting strangely with her blonde colouring. If it was a wig, its shade was a mistake. Her other accessories were in exquisite taste—exotic for a drawing room in Abersaint but they would have been perfect for the Ritz. Her terracotta dress fell in pleats from a shoestring halter, her earrings could, from their brilliance, be diamonds, and draped carelessly over one arm was a white fox fur.

Someone gasped audibly. There was a movement in the room as if sheep were suddenly aware of a dog, the people about the sofa turned and Roderick peered round them inquisitively.

'I'm so sorry I'm late,' the stranger said, 'I had trouble finding you.' She gave him a dazzling smile.

His jaw snapped shut as he remembered his manners. 'Miss Maitland! I thought you'd forgotten me. Come in, my dear, and meet my

65

guests. This,' he explained to the company who were struggling with their emotions, 'is Miss Maitland—Sandra, from the mill cottage.'

Miss Pink murmured a greeting, shook hands and drew back, her gaze wandering casually over the others. She saw that Rupert Bowen was unmistakably astonished and his wife was furious. Norman appeared both appalled and amused while Samuel seemed frankly bewildered. It was with reluctance that her eyes came round to Rachel and there she saw the same tormented hatred that the girl had displayed on the cliffs, and she could no more succeed in hiding it now than she could then.

So Miss Pink concentrated on Sandra Maitland, trying to determine if there was a man present with whom she might have formed an attachment. A cool customer, she thought; one who might choose a man like a dress: after due consideration, with confidence and without fuss. Possibly with no regard as to price. And here the confidence was of a high order. She found it impossible even to hazard as to who, if it was any of these, was Sandra's lover. For that was what Rachel had implied. It didn't have to mean that Norman Kemp had slipped the traces.

Rachel might be equally possessive about her father, her grandfather, her friend Samuel, even—she thought with a shade of amusement—in respect of the family retainer: the deferential Jones now offering the newcomer champagne with the superlative manner of a well-trained butler. Who was the victim? Was there a victim or was Rachel neurotically possessive?

CHAPTER FIVE

'WELL, I'VE *met* her,' Rupert said warily. 'Most of us have, I expect, but I had no idea that the old man knew her.'

He stood with Miss Pink at one of the windows. Behind them, raised voices held a brittle quality. Rachel was arguing with her mother about, of all things, the housekeeper's dress.

'. . . cheap and vulgar!' was Doreen's frigid comment.

'But, Mum,'—almost hysterically, 'it's all she's got! At least she dressed for the occasion.'

A burst of masculine laughter came from the direction of the sofa where Norman and Samuel stood in front of the old man and his favoured guest.

'How long has she been here?' Miss Pink asked softly.

'About six weeks—since the middle of May. They took the cottage for two months.'

'They?'

'There's a fellow: rather a rough type. Tony Thorne. He's a Londoner. They're both from London.'

'She's not what you'd expect in Abersaint.'

'Don't let my wife hear you.' He was rather drunk. 'I'm only hoping we can get through the rest of the evening without trouble. You can't trust the old man an inch. He's done it purposely, you know; mischievous old devil.'

'He's enjoying himself.'

Rupert nodded morosely. 'That's the worst of it. Did you see my wife's face?'

Miss Pink appeared not to have heard. 'She's very lovely.'

'It's not that.' He lowered his voice. 'She's been down to the pub with the fellow and d'you know what she does? Says she's tired and goes home, leaving Tony in the bar.' He goggled at her. Miss Pink's eyes were attentive. 'And a little while later,' he went on dramatically, 'we find we've lost a guest: always a well-heeled chap.'

'Lost him?'

'Gone home with her. It's incredible. Here, in Abersaint!'

'Unbelievable. Why does your—why do you put up with it?'

'Doreen's a business woman first and foremost. If she took Sandra aside and had a quiet talk with her—' Miss Pink tried to imagine this, and failed, '—next evening Sandra would walk in, large as life, with Tony in

69

tow, and open those big blue eyes at Doreen and say: "But sweetie, you didn't *mean* it!" Doreen's not going to risk a confrontation in front of the guests. We're always crowded. Besides, she's enormously popular. Well, look at her!'

'Daddy!' Rachel approached. 'Can't you do something?' Her eyes were hot and angry.

Rupert licked his lips. 'What's the matter now? What's wrong?'

'Oh, come off it. Get rid of that—that—' She turned on Miss Pink wildly. 'She's the one I was telling you about. It's obvious, isn't it?' Her voice dropped. 'Mum will make a scene, Daddy.' It was a threat.

Rupert drew himself up. 'She'll do nothing of the kind, and nor will you. Whatever's got into you? Roderick always has too much to drink at his parties. We'll be going soon,' he added lamely. 'Roderick will be tired.' He looked hard at Miss Pink.

'It's a long evening for a man of his age,' she agreed with composure. 'I think I should make a move.'

'For God's sake, don't go yet!' Rachel hissed.

'Now look—' Rupert's eyes were jumping.

But the group about the sofa was breaking up. Doreen settled herself beside her father-in-law, and Sandra crossed the room, smiling at Miss Pink.

'I love your stories,' she began, 'Roderick's been telling me who you are. I read everything you write. All those creepy houses and the lovely lady trapped by villains. I devour them.'

'Thank you.' Miss Pink was uneasy. 'It's encouraging to find an attentive reader.'

'Oh, I'm a fan! You must come and see my cottage: it's just your scene. It's the cutest place, isn't it, Rupert? Come and have coffee tomorrow.'

Rachel said coldly: 'Where's your friend tonight?'

Rupert coughed and moved aside, ostensibly making way for Samuel but continuing to retreat in the direction of his son-in-law.

'Tony went to the pub,' Sandra said carelessly.

'Does he know you're out?'

'I was wondering, Rachel,' Samuel put in earnestly, his hand on the girl's arm, 'don't you think we should get Roderick to bed? His breathing—' He hesitated, his eyes signalling frantically to Miss Pink.

'Is he not feeling well?' she asked with feigned anxiety, accepting the cue.

'You must make pots of money,' Rachel said, staring blankly at Sandra.

71

'This frock? Do you like it?'

'How much do you charge?'

'They charge? Oh, I suppose this cost—'

'I said: how much do *you* charge?'

There was a terrible silence, then: 'Aren't you a little out of your depth, sweetie?' Sandra asked in gentle reproof.

For a second Rachel was stunned, then her shoulder dropped under the blue chiffon and Miss Pink stepped forward interposing her considerable bulk.

'Rachel, I want to ask you—' She put a firm arm round the girl and steered her towards the door.

'I'm not—'

This is crucial,' hissed Miss Pink. 'Think of your grandfather. He's had enough excitement. . . .' They were safe in the hall. She drew breath. 'No scene, please. Let's keep our cool in the face of the—opposition. If you can't bear to go back and face her, then stay out of the room and I'll have a word with your mother and we'll break up the party. But your grandfather's the first consideration. You don't want him to have a stroke, do you? And with the wine he's had, and the rich food—'

Rachel gave a strangled gasp and broke away. As Miss Pink moved to block her return to the drawing room, the girl rushed upstairs.

Halfway, she stumbled and lost a sandal. She stooped to retrieve it, then hurled it at the landing. The heel cracked against panelling. She continued blindly, pulling herself up by the balusters. Miss Pink sat down heavily on the stairs.

From the drawing room came Roderick's barking laugh—which indicated that he'd fail to notice the abrupt exit of his granddaughter. She collected herself, stood up and smoothed her dress. After a moment she returned to the party and Doreen, who had been watching the door, stood up immediately and crossed the room.

'Is Rachel all right?'

'She has a bad headache and she's gone to her room to lie down. I think it's time I left.'

'No.' It was deliberate. 'Roderick,' she went on quickly, 'won't let that woman leave yet. When you go, you must take her with you.' They regarded each other intently. 'This is very embarrassing,' Doreen admitted, 'I only met you tonight but you see how it is—' she glanced at the men contemptuously, '—broken reeds, all of them. I'm depending on you to break this thing up. Hardly etiquette, is it?' She was bitter. 'Hardly the urbane celebration you were invited to?'

'Practical jokes have a way of back-firing,'

Miss Pink murmured. 'I don't think Roderick was aware of the trouble he might cause.'

'Apparently he's been ringing her up while he was in bed and talking to her! Would you credit it? He's senile.'

'I'll stay for a while but she's not doing any harm, and he's happy. My guess is that he'll tire very quickly now. We've only got to wait.'

'He'll invite her here again.'

Miss Pink shrugged. 'Rupert says her lease only has two weeks to run.'

Doreen envisaged this and her temper mounted. 'I'll make sure she doesn't come here again; I'll give her notice tomorrow. I manage the cottages, not Roderick. She can take me to court if she likes. I'd enjoy it.'

'On what grounds would you give her notice?'

'Surely you realise what she is? Why, she takes men—'

'Rupert told me.'

'Well, then?'

'That wouldn't sound nice in court.'

'As if I care!'

'Melinda!' Roderick shouted. 'Come over here! Listen to this.'

Miss Pink approached diffidently. At the old man's side Sandra regarded her with wide eyes, like a child uncertain of its reception.

'She's writing a book!' Roderick crowed.

The room was hushed and the other men were staring at the girl as if hypnotized. Doreen said lightly: 'Do tell, dear; not the story of your life?'

'The other half, Doreen,' Roderick chuckled. 'Oh, but this is too good to be true. Tell them, m'dear.'

Samuel said quickly: 'It could spoil a book to talk about it before it's finished; it might go sour on you. Do you think you ought to publicise it? What would your agent say?'

'Don't be like that.' Sandra made a roguish face at him and Miss Pink's eyes narrowed. The cool confidence of her entrance was gone and she was flushed and excited. She held an empty brandy glass on her knee but the others were too interested to notice the hint. 'The book's about finished anyway,' she went on, 'and we're all friends here, right?' Her eyes rested on Doreen. 'I like money,' she said, 'don't you?'

'I work for it.'

'So do I, sweetie.'

'This book,' Roderick said loudly, 'is about politics—politicians, rather.' He chuckled again. It was becoming irritating. He caught Miss Pink's eye and was embarrassed. 'Anyone can write a book,' he muttered, 'always be someone to supply a demand.'

'So—' Doreen exclaimed, 'you've written the story of your life and it's about politicians. Let me guess. Scandal in high places, is that it? It's been done before, and it can be very interesting indeed: exposing the private lives of prominent men. You're on to a good thing.'

'You know what?' Roderick couldn't contain himself. 'This book will bring down the government!'

There were exclamations of protest, of horrified amusement. Miss Pink asked in astonishment: 'You haven't mentioned *names*?'

'Oh, they're false,' Sandra told her ingenuously. 'There's libel, you see.'

Doreen said: 'So that's why you're hiding down here, wearing wigs and with a muscle man for protection. Doesn't the risk worry you?'

'Risk of what? I'm just avoiding the media until the job's finished, then we'll welcome them with open arms.'

Miss Pink said seriously: 'I agree with Samuel that you ought not to publicise this—'

'Why ever not?' Sandra asked. 'That's what it's all about: publicity.'

'We know what we're talking about.' Samuel was angry. 'You're sitting on a bomb,

76

and I'm quite sure your agent—'

'Look,' Sandra said with exaggerated patience, 'publicity is just what Julius wants—'

'*Not now!*'

'Now, or in a fortnight's time; what does it matter?' Her voice fell. 'Besides, I'm bored with it all. For Heaven's sake, you haven't got a reporter hiding in the cupboard, have you? The room's not bugged? Be your age, Sam; I just told Roderick for laughs.' She looked round the circle inquiringly. 'So who's going to tell?'

Jones slipped between them and bent over his employer, murmuring in his ear.

'Then bring him in,' Roderick exclaimed, 'I want to meet him. Your friend,' he told Sandra. 'Come to take yer home. Damme, you've only just arrived. He must have a drink with us.'

She gnawed her lip. 'He only went out for cigarettes.'

'He'll be worried about you.' Doreen smiled.

Rupert said suddenly: 'Pritchard's roof is in a bad state.'

Norman caught the ball. 'The roof of the cow-shed. Could we do it ourselves, Rod?'

Roderick blinked at them. 'Slates?' he

ventured. 'Just slates, or have the rafters gone?'

'That would be a big job, wouldn't it? Mean replacing the whole roof.'

The others hung on the words but they were all listening for steps in the passage.

Jones returned with a gangling young man in a creased denim suit. He had lank hair and cold eyes which fastened on Sandra as soon as he crossed the threshold.

'This is Tony,' she said in a high voice. 'It's Mr Bowen's birthday, Tony.' There was a warning in it.

The man looked at the glass in her hand and back to her face. He smiled crookedly.

'Been waiting for yer,' Roderick barked. 'Like to know me tenants. What'll yer have to drink?'

'I don't drink.' The voice was aggressively Cockney. He added, with more care but with a tinge of amusement: 'Many happy returns of the day, Mr Bowen.'

'Thank yer. Yer'll have to drink something. What have we got, Jones?'

Thorne turned to the man at his elbow. 'I'll have a Coke.'

Jones inclined his head. 'Certainly,'—the pause was studied—'sir.' He went out with his cat's tread.

78

'I've brought the car,' Thorne said carelessly to Sandra. 'Or were you fetched?'

She stood up shakily. 'I walked. Your drink's too strong, Roderick. I'll need the car to get back; couldn't make it under my own steam.' The words seemed out of character, as if she'd been deflated by the arrival of Thorne.

Miss Pink seated herself beside Roderick and the others moved away, except for Doreen who perched herself on the arm of the sofa on the other side of the old man. Their eyes met across him.

'*Well!*' Doreen breathed with infinite satisfaction.

'Hippy type,' Roderick growled. 'Broken up me party too. Never trust a feller who doesn't drink; probably got worse vices.'

'Like blackmail?' Doreen asked.

He shot her a startled glance. 'It *is* a bit near the knuckle,' he admitted, then he brightened: 'But it'll be a colossal embarrassment for the government; you've got to allow that, girl—end justifies the means, eh?'

'So long as she's confined her activities to the one party.' Doreen sparkled. 'You'd hardly think politicians would have that kind of money—well, not without some *other* form of corruption. She must come very expensive;

I mean, those ear-rings are diamonds, Dad. And the fur! Exquisite. And doesn't she look pretty in that dress?'

He stared at his daughter-in-law with intensity. 'She's only here for a week or two more; you've got nothing to worry about.'

Her face stiffened, then relaxed. 'I hate her guts,' she confessed, but lightly. 'However, I can still be objective. She's remarkably attractive; it's a pity she hasn't got the brains to go with it.'

'You call that objective?'

She sighed. 'It's obvious that Thorne is her protector.' She emphasised the word, raising her eyebrows at Miss Pink. 'She got away from him tonight, drank too much and talked. Look at his face. There's trouble in store for Miss Maitland.'

'She can probably hold her own with him,' Miss Pink put in. 'After all, he allows her to go—places without him on other occasions—' Roderick gaped at her, '—but I don't like the idea of this book. I wonder how many people she's told about it.'

'She never talked at the hotel,' Doreen said. 'This is the first anyone's heard of it, to my knowledge.'

'It's to be hoped it won't go any further.'

'You think she's in danger?' Roderick

80

asked unhappily.

'I'm afraid she's asked for it, Dad.' Her eyes belied the concern in her tone. She shrugged and grimaced at Miss Pink over the old man's head. 'But I've no doubt she can pull the wool over most men's eyes; that sort can get away with murder.'

CHAPTER SIX

A WEB OF paths like animal runs connected places in the village and radiated outwards to the fields. The following morning, equipped with a large-scale map, Miss Pink followed an earthy alley along the side of her garage, past parched back gardens, to a meadow where fat cows grazed among the buttercups. Ahead was a low wooded hill and when she reached the top she looked down through the trees to the valley of a minor stream. There were glimpses of a cart track and of a sunlit glade with turf running up to the white walls of a cottage. Upstream, a ruin and a rusty mill wheel rose above the alders. The scene was idyllic, flowers in the back garden of the cottage making brilliant splashes of colour against the green jungle.

She descended to the track where it crossed the stream by way of an ancient bridge. Above it the water was choked by cresses and yellow monkey flower, but below, it chattered clear under a shaven bank. Someone had been busy with a lawnmower. There was a smell of mayweed and dust, a ground hum of insects and then, from the cottage, a woman's quick laugh, without amusement. Two cars stood beside the track: a rakish red Spitfire and a battered Saab.

The cottage held an air of magic, like a place in a fairy forest. Its chimneys were tall and rounded with a pattern of diamond trellising in the plaster. There were tiny sash windows on the ground floor, skylights in the slates, and the walls were a yard thick. As Miss Pink raised her hand to knock on the open door, a man's voice said harshly: 'It's in the filing cabinet, I take it?' There was no response and he continued: 'You seem to have gone off at half-cock; you've leaked it deliberately—right? And when we follow it up, you play dumb. What's the idea?'

Miss Pink knocked. There was a moment's silence and then a tall blonde stepped back and glanced over her shoulder. She wore flared white pants and an emerald shirt and Miss Pink was about to ask for Sandra when she saw that this was Sandra, and now that the black wig had gone she looked all of a piece, and even more beguiling.

'Good morning, Miss Pink!' It was said gaily but her eyes were intent, conveying some message. 'Do come in; we're entertaining the Press—would you believe it? Two gentlemen from *The Sketch*.'

Miss Pink stepped into a dim living room and two men stood up: a portly fellow whom Sandra introduced as Mr Waterhouse, and a second, called Rogers, who nodded unhappily at her and sat down with an air of effacing himself. His companion assessed Miss Pink with shrewd eyes, remarked that it was a fine day for walking and paused for a response that might carry some interest for him. He was middle-aged and professional and she took her time about replying, surveying the room owlishly from behind her spectacles.

Sprawled in a chair by the fireplace Tony Thorne glowered at her and made no attempt to get up. Her glance passed over him to the good Welsh dresser which over-shadowed a small filing cabinet—a two-drawer job: the only features of interest in the otherwise standard furniture of a holiday cottage.

'You're busy,' she said pleasantly, 'I'll come back at a more convenient time.'

Thorne said suddenly and surprisingly: 'We want to talk to you, Sandra and me.' He looked bleakly at the reporters.

'Meaning you prefer our room to our company,' Waterhouse said. 'How long will you be? We haven't got all day.'

'No one asked you to come.'

Sandra and Waterhouse started to speak

together and stopped, staring at Miss Pink.
She moved towards the door.

'No!' Thorne stood up abruptly. 'I'm
asking you to stay.' From his tone he was
demanding it. He turned on the other men.
'You can wait outside; there are some seats up
at the end.' He jerked his head and Miss Pink
saw through a back window, seats under fruit
trees some distance away, out of earshot. 'No
pictures,' he told them coldly. 'And if you get
tired of waiting, that's fine by us.'

Waterhouse showed no sign of affront. He
stood for a moment, studying the other
thoughtfully, then turned and followed his
partner out through the back door.

'Don't needle them,' Sandra said. 'And I
don't see why we have to bother Miss Pink.'

'She's an authoress, isn't she?' He turned to
her. 'She said you write stories—miss.' She
couldn't restrain a smile. It had the effect of
encouraging him. 'We got a problem; perhaps
you can help.'

The diffidence sat badly on him. Sandra
was biting her lip and darting quick glances at
Miss Pink who wondered if Thorne knew that
the girl had talked indiscreetly last night. She
decided she must play it canny. From the
presence of the reporters it looked as if someone had talked.

85

They sat down, Sandra on a chair beside Thorne. She stared intently at the visitor.

'I've written a book,' she began.

'Yes?' Miss Pink was all bright encouragement.

'About—should I tell her, Tony?'

'Cut the cackle. She'll know as soon as she gets to the village. Everybody will know. You worried?'

'It will shock you.' The steady stare implored Miss Pink to be shocked.

Thorne said roughly: 'It's about a call-girl with a pad in Westminster—autobiography, they calls it. She knows a lot of politicians, see.' His smile was lewd.

Miss Pink was nonplussed. 'Why?'

'Why what?'

'What's the purpose behind it?'

'Money,' Sandra said. She relaxed visibly.

'It'll fetch a few thousand,' Thorne said airily.

Miss Pink looked vacuous. 'It doesn't sound very nice.' Sandra's lips twitched. 'Not at all nice,' Miss Pink continued reprovingly. 'But perhaps I have the wrong. . . . ? What kind of advice do you expect from me? On marketing?'

Thorne shifted impatiently. 'It's not finished yet; it don't seem right to tell the Press at this moment of time. It'll pre-empt the issue, right?'

Miss Pink stared at him.

'But they know!' Sandra broke in earnestly, gesturing to the garden: 'They arrived at breakfast time and they know everything already: about the book, and where I live, they even know my professional name—' she grinned mischievously, '—it's Cynthia Gale.'

Miss Pink frowned; she hadn't told them that last night. 'So what did you say to them?'

'Well, I had to admit it, didn't I? I've got to go along with my agent; he's the brains. He's planned a fabulous publicity campaign: telly, papers, magazines, the lot—only thing wrong is he didn't warn us he was ready to start.'

'What does he say about that?' Miss Pink's tone was idle; she wasn't really interested. She wanted to get away.

'I can't get him,' Thorne said, 'I been trying since these guys arrived. We got this contact, see, and he says Jul— our agent's in France. We knew that but we thought he must have come back with the Press coming here, and that, but I guess he could have rung *The Sketch* just as well from Paris.'

'The telephone systems do connect.' Sandra was sarcastic.

'If he's abroad, he's got to have rung from

there, ain't he?' He was vicious. 'Unless he left the job to someone else: to do while he was away.'

'Yes,' Sandra said. 'He could have done that.'

'Has he not got in touch with you?' Miss Pink asked. They stared at her blankly. 'No; silly question. And you can't get him this morning.' Her eyes went to the telephone on the dresser. 'Perhaps he can't find a telephone.' She regarded them blandly. 'What were his plans?'

Thorne's eyes narrowed but he made no move to stop Sandra when she said that the plan had been to secure serialisation rights for the proposed book in continental publications. This elusive agent was now concerned with marketing in Paris, Bonn, Rome. Miss Pink had a sudden vision of rock and air and sparkling sea, she smelt the coconut smell of gorse. She stood up and saw consternation in Sandra's eyes.

'The only thing I can suggest is that you stall the Press until you've contacted your agent; you might even tell them that: no comment until you have his instructions. You can suggest he's the boss—' it was dryly put for it was obvious that Sandra had no hand in the plot of this thing; she just wrote the book. 'Of course,' Miss Pink added slyly, 'you'd do better to go into hiding again: Manchester perhaps, since you're known in London.'

'We can find a safe place in London,' Thorne said quickly, then: 'Why should we? We're meant to get publicity.'

'Quite. I'm sorry I couldn't be of more assistance. . . .' The hypocrisy came easily; a ritual leave-taking kept the thing superficial, or was meant to. She didn't want her day spoiled by a nasty taste in the mouth. All the same, as she went on her way she felt that for all Sandra's beauty and Thorne's arrogance, perhaps because of them, these two had an air that was more Babes in the Wood than villains. And already, before she'd climbed out of the miniature valley, another car was nosing down the track and over the bridge to halt outside the cottage, another pair got out in flared pants and drip-dry shirts, and cameras glinted in the sun. Silly girl, she thought.

★   ★   ★

It was late when she reached the summit of Carn Goch. She explored the Bronze Age fort from a sense of duty but the foundations of hut circles evoked no sense of time, still less any feeling of involvement with the people who lived here two thousand years ago. After a cursory examination she ensconced herself on the crumbling ramparts to eat her lunch. She had chosen the southern portal and the whole of the peninsula was spread before her, with Riffli's woods on the left, the headland in front, and close below, under the scarp of the mountain, the farm called Corn, bright and abandoned as seen through the binoculars, with not even a hen abroad in the glare of its empty yard.

Pritchard was the farmer's name, she remembered. He was hay-making; the whine of the tractor drifting through honey-scented air, counterpoint to the drone of bees in heather. In the next field to the tractor skirted figures toiled: advancing, retreating, bowing before a black toad-shape—the Pritchard women, presumably, raking hay round the Corn cromlech.

When she'd finished her lunch she turned, settled herself comfortably again and focused on the mill cottage which, as the raven flew, was a mile away.

She looked up the course of the millstream to the west gable. The place appeared busy in the early afternoon. There were a number of cars on the track but what she took to be the Spitfire now stood on the bank of the stream and, full in the sun's glare, was a large white car which might well be the Bowens' Mercedes.

Someone was making passes over the Spitfire—if it was the Spitfire—and this puzzled her until she realised the car was being washed. The person concerned was blue below and brown on top—a man in jeans and without a shirt? Thorne? But another, dressed similarly, stood stationary where a person might stand if he were talking to people sitting in the shade of the fruit trees in the garden.

Someone dressed in white passed under the gable-end and paused by the Spitfire. After a moment she—surely this was Doreen—went to the Mercedes, got in, and the big car moved away down the track.

The scene had the lazy quality of a dream; one had no inkling of what was being said, and broader gestures were invisible. People moved and halted, a car ran into a tunnel formed by trees and reappeared as in a film with the sound track cut. But there was sound. She lowered the binoculars and heard the bees and the rasp of a dry wind on the baking stones. She packed her rucksack and set off down the scarp towards the cliffs and the birds which went about their business, made no demands and yet were beautiful.

There were times when one needed animals as an antidote to human beings.

*   *   *

She walked right round the peninsula, seeing no one other than a few visitors and none of these ventured out to the headland. She returned to the village to swim in the limpid sea and at six o'clock she made her way to the hotel.

From behind the bar Rupert greeted her with circumspection, his eyes flickering to the customers: an affluent middle-aged pair in blazers and club ties discussing trust funds.

'Have you heard?' he whispered.

'Sandra?'

'What a to-do!' He was bubbling with excitement. 'A couple of reporters came in for lunch. Of course, she knew it was going to be leaked last night, didn't she? Telling us was a kind of trailer.' His eyes danced. 'There's a television team on the way; they tried to book rooms but we're full.'

'Have they contacted the agent yet?'

'They don't need an agent; they're doing very well on their own, from all I hear. I only hope we can keep the media away from Roderick; he does so love being on the box. We had a dose of it during the campaign. Once he gets in front of the cameras, there's no knowing what he might say—' He stopped short. After a moment he added flatly: 'We're running a business here; our kind of guest might not like scandal. Sandra, I mean.'

'Don't tell me you have other scandals in Abersaint.' It was flippant and it didn't reach him. She added, seriously: 'I don't see why the Press should seek out Roderick; he's only the owner of the mill cottage and, technically, Sandra is nothing more than his tenant.'

'Quite.' He was quick, and a little flustered. 'Of course, we make no secret of her having been here, but only as a customer.' He avoided her eye. 'We had no idea what was going on.'

'Naturally. And as soon as she leaves, the Press will follow her: a nine-days wonder— less, one would hope.'

More people came in the bar, putting an end to private conversation. Miss Pink drew back from the counter and listened to the highly volatile remarks of the guests. The grapevine had been at work. The ladies were agog, the men speculative, but everyone was excited. Predictably, it was the human aspect of the situation that enthralled the feminine element: 'She was in this bar at the weekend,

93

and a pearl comb in her hair, my dear, and her dress! Pale green shantung. ... What? Oh, you remember *shantung*. ...'

The men were concerned with the repercussions in high places. 'Shouldn't wonder if it'll affect the market, old man; if the government falls—'

'Never!'

'What else? They've only the most slender majority ... a vote of confidence. ...'

Doreen appeared in the doorway, in long black and white cotton with a scarlet belt. She caught Miss Pink's eye and came over.

'I'm going to have my dinner early to escape the crowd. Would you care to join me? Rupert can't leave the bar. ...'

They sat at a table in the window and talked about currents and safe beaches until the waiter came with iced cucumber soup. Doreen stubbed out her cigarette.

'Has Rupert told you the news?'

'Yes, and I was up there this morning.'

'How many reporters were there then?'

'Two. One would be a photographer.'

'I went up after lunch and there were half a dozen: getting on with her like a house on fire—more or less. Thorne was a drag: not letting her out of his sight in case she got at the brandy, is my guess. She was drinking beer.'

'Did you give her notice?'

'How could I—with the Press flapping their ears? I asked what her plans were though and she told me, as brazenly as you please, that the book would be finished in a fortnight and then she'd go back to London— in other words, she's staying out her term. I went to Riffli and blew my top. You can guess Roderick's reaction; he said he'd have her up to tea tomorrow and persuade her it's in her own interests to go. You know what that means! She'll be at Riffli every day and all day for the next fortnight. He's bewitched. Isn't there some legal pressure we could bring to bear to force her to go?'

'Anything like an accusation of running a disorderly house would rebound on you.' Miss Pink was dry. 'But my guess is that they'll go within the week.'

'You haven't talked to her about it. She's an arrogant bitch.'

'Were the Press interested when you asked if she was leaving?'

'Not so that you'd notice. It was a very public conversation: out in the garden. Rather unworldly, I thought.' Miss Pink showed surprise. 'Heat,' Doreen explained, 'and all the reporters were getting tight; it reminded me of an old French film.' She leaned across the table, lowering her voice. 'They were discussing "presents" which, I gather, are a bonus over and above what are known as "basics". Apparently if you're in an upper bracket and you can count Arabs and such among your customers, the sky's the limit.' She regarded her wine thoughtfully. 'An opossum coat was mentioned—*and* its price: just on a thousand.'

'How did the Press react to that?'

'It was laid on for them, wasn't it? They made notes—and they watched me to see how I was taking it.'

'Did she mention any names in regard to the people in the book?'

'There was something about an "Uncle Tom", and a wog called Ahmed who was something to do with oil and was responsible for the opossum coat but she pointed out that those weren't their real names. It was a repetition of last night—a little more sordid in view of the company.'

'What will you do if she comes down to the hotel?'

'Good Lord, you're not suggesting she'd do that!' In the face of Miss Pink's silence Doreen was forced to consider this and horror gave way to speculation. She nodded slowly and smiled. 'She'd be good for trade—and with everyone watching her, none of the residents, even the unattached ones, would dare to go outside the bar with her, let alone back to the cottage.'

'How devious of you.'

Doreen preened herself. 'I must admit that when I went up there after lunch I was hell-bent on a flaming row and when I saw young Jakey washing her car, I almost turned back, I was so furious. After all, Jakey's only fourteen. But I had to see how things were going, so I decided to play it off the cuff. Then, when she'd given me a drink and they'd started on the fur coat bit, and I watched their eyes, I realised that all I had to do was to play along with her. Give her enough rope and she'll hang herself. If she comes down here and talks the same way, no one's going to touch her with a barge-pole, but no one.'

'Very shrewd,' Miss Pink murmured. 'What was Jakey Jones doing there?'

Doreen was too preoccupied to ask her how she'd come to meet Jakey. 'He's by way of being her odd-job boy—what an unhealthy sound that's got in the circumstances! Cuts the grass and so on. Not that I'm worried about Jakey; I doubt if even she can corrupt him any more. He's beyond parental control;

most of the petty theft and vandalism in Aber-saint can be traced back to Jakey or Oswald Hughes. Myfanwy Hughes has been most un-fortunate. I don't know whether it's worse not to know who your father is, like Ossie, or to have one who thinks he's the Lord's Anoint-ed, like Caradoc Jones. So—' she finished evilly, '—Jakey has gravitated naturally to the mill cottage. I understand there's a strong link between prostitution and crime; some-thing to do with social outcasts?'

'No doubt. Someone said last night that Samuel was a frequent visitor at the mill cot-tage.'

'Did they? He has curious tastes. He wasn't there this afternoon.'

'What does he do?'

Doreen looked at the sun on the water. 'I think you should ask him.' There was no hos-tility in her tone. Miss Pink tried another line.

'What's Rachel got against Sandra?'

'What has anyone?' After a pause she quali-fied this. 'She's jealous of Samuel going up there; he's an old family friend. And she's highly strung. She's—on—tranquillisers, at the moment. You have to understand that the nuclear power business took an awful lot out of us, out of Rachel most particularly.' The sentences were jerked out of her as if she were retreating, step by step, through defences. Her distaste for the subject was in sharp contrast to her acid volubility in respect of her visit to the mill cottage, and with the arrival of the main course she started to talk about gourmet dishes and stubbornly resisted all attempts on Miss Pink's part to revert to personalities.

They separated after dinner and Miss Pink was sitting over a quiet brandy in the bar when someone said jovially: 'Will you have another of those, Miss Pink?' It was the large reporter whom she'd met at the cottage.

He saw her effort at recall. 'Waterhouse was the name. Allow me to buy you a brandy.'

She didn't protest. He wanted to talk, and the mechanics of this situation were intriguing. He returned with whisky and brandy.

'Cheers!'

'Your very good health.'

He sighed comfortably, settled his chins and peered at her. 'I'm too fat for this heat.' She looked sympathetic. He went on, with studied carelessness: 'They'd have been picking your brains this morning: how to handle the publicity angle. I know who you are, you see; checked up. Gothics, isn't it? My wife reads 'em. You must find this business interesting—not to put too fine a point on it. Come up with any advice?'

'To contact their agent.' She was equable.

'Only thing you could say, wasn't it? He's still missing though.'

'Perhaps he's abroad—or in transit.'

He nodded. 'In transit, abroad. He'll be back when the story breaks. Someone's double-crossed him.'

'What makes you think that?'

'Obvious. No, not obvious, but highly likely. Look: the leak didn't originate with him because he'd have warned them. Besides, the timing's wrong; she wasn't meant to be run to earth at this point. They weren't ready for us. So someone other than the agent tipped off the Press; someone trying to throw a spanner in the works.'

'What could be the motive for that?'

He raised massive shoulders. 'Who knows?'

'What form did the leak take?'

'Telephone call last night: at half twelve. No chance of tracing it, of course. It was received at our Fleet Street office and the chap who took it can't say whether the caller was a man or a woman. The message was that there was a t— a lady calling herself Sandra Maitland, professional name Cynthia Gale, writing a book that would make headlines, that she had a flat in Westminster but was

100

living down here under this assumed name.'

'Did you tell Sandra this?'

'No.' He shot her a glance. 'She might not have said so much if she'd known it wasn't her agent made the call.'

Miss Pink said at length. 'I don't see what they stand to gain.'

'Who? Sandra?'

'No. This person who rang your office. Could it be revenge: to stop her making a lot of money? But she can still make it. The book exists—presumably—and can be sold when she's finished it. What was the point of that call?'

'You worry too much.' He hadn't really been listening. 'I'm not worried. The story's coming along nicely; we're digging. She talked quite a lot this afternoon. She *is* a call-girl and there is a book, no doubt on that score. My editor had the bright idea of ringing round the publishers and they've found one who's actually seen the first couple of chapters. They turned it down flat. The book exists all right, but it's too hot to handle.'

CHAPTER SEVEN

THE B.B.C. MADE no mention of Sandra on the eight o'clock news programme next morning. Miss Pink was not surprised. She was grinding her coffee when Roderick rang and asked her to take him to the mill cottage. He sounded subdued. She nodded sagely at the receiver.

'You've lost your tenants.'

'God! Who told you?'

Over-playing it, she thought; dragging the last bit of relish from the situation. She was short with him. 'Sandra was a liability and you're well rid of her. If—'

'You don't know what you're saying.'

She spelled it out for him. 'The village would suffer in the long run with that kind of publicity. One good thing: they'll have taken the Press away with them. . . . I suppose you want me to see in what kind of state they've left the place: check the contents against the inventory, is that it?'

There was silence at the other end of the line. She was about to ask if he were still there when he said ominously: 'I want you to meet me on the Riffli track and take me up to the mill.'

She sighed. She had been looking forward to a full day on the headland. 'Why me, Roderick? Can't one of the family take you? I have no authority if they've walked off with articles, you know; it would be a police job.'

'No, Mel, this is not about stolen articles. It's rather worse than that, d'you see. The place burned down in the night.'

She gaped at the telephone. 'What place?'

'The mill cottage.'

'I don't—' She checked. After a moment she asked: 'Was someone—injured?'

'There's some doubt on that score. I'll start walking now; you come up the track and meet me.'

She met him in Riffli's woods: a gnome-like figure in climbing breeches, walking with the help of a stick. She backed the Austin among the bluebells and turned. He got in beside her, his face stiff.

'Did they get out?' she asked, before he'd settled himself.

'Keep going; I don't want the others to know where I've gone.' She threw a quizzical glance at him but engaged gear. 'They're too young,' he said lamely, then with more spirit: 'Rachel is.'

'They were—*are*—in the cottage?'

'There's no car outside the place.'

'In that case, they've gone: nipped away in the night to dodge the reporters. That's obvious.' Her words seemed to echo in the ensuing silence.

He stared through the windscreen as they descended to the village, crossed the bridge and turned up the main valley. After a few hundred yards, when they were in the trees, he said: 'Turn right in a moment.'

She did so and found herself on an unsurfaced track. Still he said nothing. She didn't like that.

'Who discovered the fire?'

He stirred. 'Some television people. Came up here about nine o'clock this morning. She made the appointment with them last night.'

'What did they have to say?'

'Don't know, in detail. They told the police there'd been a fire; the police rang me. They say the chap who reported it on the phone sounded odd. Shocked.'

The track dipped to the bridge but the cottage was screened by foliage bowed above the car. Then the gradient levelled and there was the green glade, the white walls, but less white now, and bare rafters like a charred rib cage. Wisps of smoke rose from the interior into a translucent sky. Only the trellised chimneys were untouched.

They crossed the turf to the place where the door had been. The sun was blasting down on the glade but Miss Pink felt cold. She remembered her companion's age.

'We'll wait for the police,' she said firmly. He took no notice.

They stood in the doorway. The stairs had collapsed, and the bedroom floors. In the desolation lay two sets of bedsprings, the metal discernible among fallen slates. That on the left was narrow but the other was the remains of a double bed. There was something more than slates on this.

Miss Pink said carefully: 'It's impossible to tell.'

'We have to face it, Mel.'

'Yes.'

She forced her brain to concentrate but still she stared for some time before she continued, with the same careful enunciation which was not so much the result of a thought process as an interpretation of images: 'Yes, that has some relation to a human shape . . . and that might be a hand. But what else would you expect to find on a bed?'

She touched his arm. Tacitly they turned and stepped out into the sunlight. She removed her spectacles and wiped her eyes which were smarting from the smoke. They walked to the bridge and sat on the parapet listening to the water. A pied wagtail flirted on the bank.

'Which one is it?' he asked.

They looked at each other.

'The Spitfire's gone,' she said.

'What does it mean, Mel?'

A police car came down the track and stopped on the bridge. They regarded the occupants without interest. Another car, unmarked, crept up behind.

'Morning, Mr Bowen.' The sergeant in the first car was alert and cheery; he would have seen a lot of shock. 'You've been inside?'

'Yes.'

'Is there someone——?'

'I'm afraid so.'

The man nodded. 'These chaps said as much.' He indicated the second car. Miss Pink realised that this was the television team. 'A bad business,' the sergeant said. 'We'll park the car.'

The men in the second car stared blankly ahead as they passed. They looked frightened.

The two policemen walked across the turf to the cottage. The birds in the woods seemed very loud. The watchers stood immobile. No one spoke.

After a while the police emerged from the singed doorway and the constable went quickly round the gable-end. Someone sighed heavily. Miss Pink yawned. The sergeant looked at the trees and eased his collar. He wiped his hands with his handkerchief and kept on wiping them as he approached. The television men took a step nearer. The sergeant halted and stared at Roderick with shocked eyes.

'Not as bad as it looks,' the old man said easily. 'Asphyxiation first; remember yer First Aid. Unconscious by the time the fire gets to them.'

'You think so?' It could have been a child speaking.

'Yer see a lot worse in motor accidents. It's all over; got to get on with the formalities.'

'Yes, sir.'

'Me daughter-in-law will have her address. Name was Sandra Maitland. Don't know the age.' He paused.

Miss Pink turned away. Poor fellow; despite Roderick's assurance, motor accidents were no kind of preparation for what lay on that bedspring—unless they involved burned-out vehicles.

She drove Roderick back to the village. Alone in the car, he repeated his question.

'What do you make of it?'

'I haven't had a chance to think.'

'First impressions then.'

She slowed for a string of dry potholes. 'A lot of people die in bed: smoking, drinking. She drank brandy; that's highly inflammable.'

'Where's Thorne?'

'And the Spitfire. The first impression is that he took it.'

'That's what I thought.' After a while he asked: 'Why?'

'Either he escaped from the fire,' she said slowly, 'or he wasn't there when it started. He came back to find the place burning, couldn't save her, and he drove away. . . . He couldn't face a police investigation—because of his background. He may have a record.'

'That seems a likely explanation.'

'I can't think of any other.'

This was untrue. Her mind refused to contemplate any other.

*   *   *

'How do you know Thorne escaped? There could be a second body under the debris.'

They were in the Bowens' sitting room on the first floor of the hotel. The younger

Bowens had listened to the account of the disaster with mounting horror and then Doreen put the question about Thorne.

'We'll know soon enough,' Rupert told her with distaste. 'They'll send forensic people down.'

'But if there are two bodies,' she insisted, 'who took the Spitfire?'

Roderick, looking lost in the middle of a huge settee, glanced at Miss Pink. 'What's Ted Roberts' number?'

'He's in the Pyrenees,' she reminded him. 'He won't be back until next week.'

'You think we need him?' Rupert was doubtful. 'What's wrong with your own man?'

'*No!*' It was wrenched out of Doreen. She put her fingers to her lips, then asked coldly: 'What on earth do we want with a solicitor?'

No one answered her. On the leads outside the window a gull cleared its throat and gave a tentative scream. The sound of the holiday makers rose to them, and the long wash of the sea.

'I'll make some coffee,' Doreen said without expression. 'We'll need some sustenance if the police are on the way.' She looked towards Miss Pink but not at her and her eyes were stark with horror. When she'd gone, Rupert brought brandy and glasses from a corner cupboard, apologising for not thinking of it before. He started to talk desultorily about insurance and the question of rebuilding the cottage while Roderick studied his knees and Miss Pink's gaze ranged the room, attracted by colour but not really absorbing it. The settee and armchairs were in white leather, the carpet was beige; there was blue glassware on perspex shelves. It was a light modern room without much character and would have been most impracticable with open fires. She winced at the thought.

Doreen returned with the coffee. Rupert, about to close the door behind her, stopped short at the appearance of the angular receptionist.

'There's two gentlemen, Mr Bowen—'

A voice Miss Pink recognised greeted Rupert with a genial 'Good morning, Mr Bowen!' and Detective Superintendent Pryce walked into the room with the solid assurance of a man whose job gave him the right to be there without invitation. He was followed by Sergeant Williams. She'd met them when they'd investigated the murders at her own adventure centre. [*Lady With a Cool Eye*]

Roderick knew Pryce and, without rising, he barked introductions from the settee.

'We've met Miss Pink,' Pryce said, shaking her hand. 'They told me you were here, ma'am. Tragedies follow you around, don't they?' He smiled deprecatingly. 'I see Mr Roberts occasionally; seems you've had your fill of criminals lately, one way and another. Now, what have we here?'

He sat down, accepted a cup of coffee and regarded them cordially. Williams seated himself at the table. His hand moved to his pocket and came away empty. His lined face grew more lugubrious as he tried to make his own decision regarding the taking of notes. Pryce ignored him.

The superintendent was a florid rubbery man, balding and with a paunch. Neither looked healthy, nor even very effectual but a closer study of Pryce revealed that his eyes were not in the least jolly despite the fruity voice, the expansive manner. He was observing Roderick.

'A nasty shock for you, sir. They told me you were up there. With Miss Pink.'

The old man stirred. 'Friend of the family,' he mumbled.

'I'm on holiday,' she contributed. 'I've taken a cottage in the village.' Why did she have to justify herself? Because everyone felt a measure of guilt in the presence of the

111

police?

'Why C.I.D.?' Roderick asked, his head on one side like a chaffinch.

'Sir? What did you expect?'

'But it was an accident!' Rupert exclaimed.

'Faulty wiring?'

'The place was all re-wired last winter,' Roderick said flatly.

'Not faulty wiring then.' They stared at Pryce, fascinated. Miss Pink had the feeling of being caught up in pre-ordained events. She didn't realise that she was still shocked. 'We were interested in your tenants before we heard about the fire,' Pryce was saying. 'You'd expect that, wouldn't you?' He beamed at them and Doreen nodded quickly. 'You've seen the papers, of course.' The tone was conversational. Rupert said yes, they'd seen the papers but Miss Pink and Roderick shook their heads; they hadn't had time. 'So,' Pryce continued, 'I found that very interesting indeed, particularly as it's on my patch. A call-girl writing her memoirs, involving prominent men—' he looked shocked, '—a bit off-centre, that. I was on the phone to *The Sketch* when news came in about the fire, not to speak of some question that there might be a body in the cottage. I thought it was worth a trip down here.' He looked at them blandly.

112

'And when we get here, we find one person missing—and the car.' There was a pause. 'The book's gone too,' he added.

Miss Pink recovered first. 'How can you tell?'

'It was in a filing cabinet, or so the papers said. That had a beam across it but the beam wasn't holding anything up so we moved it and opened the cabinet—which wasn't locked. There was nothing inside.'

'But there wouldn't be—' Rupert caught his wife's eye and subsided.

'There'd be charred paper,' Pryce said. 'There was nothing.'

'Thorne ran off with it, eh?' Roderick sounded as if he were trying to be helpful.

'Someone has, sir.'

'Is it not possible,' Miss Pink ventured, 'that Sandra was reading this book—or manuscript—in bed?'

'No, ma'am.' He was unexpectedly firm. They all felt the change and their attention sharpened. 'At eleven o'clock,' he went on, 'the television men left. They'd arrived late and she said she was far too tired to give them an interview then. She told them to come back at nine this morning. They said she looked exhausted. They left her and the Thorne fellow clearing up after the party

113

they'd had. From what they say the girl was far too tired to take any book to bed with her.'

'What you mean is: she was dead drunk.' Doreen was icy.

'Not at all; she was cold sober.'

'At eleven?' Miss Pink asked suddenly.

'At eleven.' He looked expectant.

'I don't know when the fire started. . . .' She glanced at him but he gave her no help. 'But I—we were thinking in terms of an accident involving brandy and smoking in bed. You don't think so?'

He raised his shoulders. 'There's a lot to do yet. When did the fire start? Where? When was the book removed from the filing cabinet?' His eyes rested on Roderick. 'Why was it taken? Where was the Spitfire at eleven o'clock?'

After a moment Miss Pink said stupidly: 'I beg your pardon?'

'The television chaps were the last to leave—no, so far as they know, they were the last. At that moment the couple were in the kitchen clearing up and the T.V. men saw themselves out. The reason that they thought everyone else was gone was that theirs was the only car out front. No Spitfire. In fact, they'd seen no Spitfire when they arrived.'

'What time was that?' Miss Pink asked.

114

'Around ten-thirty. People were leaving then.'

'Then who took the Spitfire?' Rupert asked.

Pryce didn't look worried. 'Thorne probably took it and hid it while the party was in progress.'

'Why?' Miss Pink asked.

Pryce looked at Williams, who spoke for the first time. He cleared his throat. 'Most likely reason would be so the lady inside wouldn't hear him start the engine, miss.'

She blinked at him. Everyone looked bewildered, except Pryce.

'Do you have the registration number of the Spitfire?' he asked. No one had. 'No matter. Have you Thorne's address?' The Bowens shook their heads.

'I have Sandra's,' Doreen volunteered.

'We have that, ma'am.'

'Has Thorne got a record?' Rupert asked.

Pryce looked sly. 'We're checking on that.' He couldn't resist adding: 'And a lot of other things.'

Doreen was saying: 'I never trusted that man; he was so obviously mercenary.'

'You knew him, ma'am?'

'Naturally. They drank here. I'm not at all surprised at what's happened; I mean:

115

stealing the book—and the car. That must have been worth quite a bit. And then,' she added smugly, 'no innocent survivor of a fire would run away.'

'You thought he could be a villain?'

'I wouldn't say he impressed me as being honest. What would you say, darling?' Rupert sucked in his cheeks thoughtfully and shook his head.

'Rough,' he asserted, 'very rough. I'd never have employed him anywhere near a till. You can tell, you know: there's a look in the eyes. . . .'

'And what did you think of him, sir?' Pryce turned on Roderick, now slumped on the settee like an empty sack. His pale eyes looked beyond the superintendent.

'Didn't drink. Never trust a feller who doesn't drink. No manners either; that's what's wrong with this country. . . .' His head drooped. Doreen sighed.

'How did you come to meet him?' Pryce's tone was sharp.

Roderick roused himself. 'Come to me party last—when was it? Tuesday. Last Tuesday. I was eighty-seven.'

'Congratulations, sir.'

'Came along in a temper to take the girl home; didn't like her being out on her own.'

'You invited her to your party?'

'Dammit, she was me tenant!'

'Of course,' Doreen put in earnestly, 'none of us, least of all my father-in-law, had any idea what she *was*. She was our mystery woman: ravishingly beautiful; you should have seen her. I daresay you'll see photographs but they won't do her justice. She was so vital! Such a scandal for Abersaint.' Her face fell. 'It's not amusing, is it? Not any longer. I still can't believe it's happened. Poor child; she was being manipulated.'

'What makes you say that, ma'am?'

'It was obvious. It's not hindsight, I assure you; I remarked on it to Miss Pink. I mean: she was dim, empty-headed; she was completely under his thumb.'

'Whose?'

'Why, Thorne's. He was her—what do you call it?—protector? In every sense of the word.'

'We didn't know that,' Rupert put in quickly.

'No; I said: this is hindsight. All we knew was that she was beautiful, not very bright—and an alcoholic.'

'Indeed?' Pryce looked at Miss Pink.

'Brandy,' she contributed. 'And she couldn't hold it; not at Mr Bowen's party

117

anyway. I think one of Thorne's duties would be to keep her sober.'

'What did you think of him, ma'am?'

Miss Pink assembled her observations. 'He had the air of a petty criminal but he was careful, within his limits. He had no experience outside his job, if one assumes that to be some kind of bodyguard. He was confounded by the arrival of the reporters. I'd say he was in a panic yesterday.'

'What—all day?'

'He had himself under control when I was there in the afternoon,' Doreen put in. 'I'd say he was angry, alert; suspicious, yes, but not panicking.' She looked inquiringly towards Miss Pink.

Rupert said slowly: 'His subsequent behaviour doesn't show panic. He hid the car where no one would see it, came back, stole the book from the cabinet, walked to where he'd hidden the car. . . . Ah, that's why he hid it: he had to get his possessions out of the cottage without her noticing, so he got them out while the party was on.' He beamed, not seeing that their faces were closed against him. 'And then he drove away!'

'You forgot something,' Pryce said.

'What?'

'The fire.'

For a moment Rupert was taken aback, then he resumed sulkily: '*I* think she was drinking and smoking in bed. So she was tired: that's just when you need a pick-me-up, and having had one, she'd go on—particularly if she was an alcoholic. It was a coincidence certainly—' his eyes came round slowly, very slowly to his wife and, for the first time, he became aware of her expression, '—wasn't it?' he whispered. The words slipped out and he made a quick movement as if they were tangible and he could grab them back.

Pryce said smoothly; 'There's more than one apparent coincidence here. The book disappearing at the same time as the fire is one, but those two things happened only twenty-four hours after the story was leaked to the Press. The lady lived down here for six weeks without anything happening, then suddenly, everything happens.'

'But the agent leaked the story deliberately,' Doreen said.

'Yes?' Pryce looked vacuous. 'But it was so useful to Thorne, wasn't it? All those reporters at the cottage, getting in each other's way, no doubt; cars rushing here and there, so no one missed the Spitfire being driven away—almost certainly in the dark—yes, it

119

must have been. Doesn't it seem likely that the leak was a ploy to lure a lot of people to the cottage?'

'Why?' Doreen asked carelessly.

'As cover.'

'For what?'

'The theft of the book. It could be worth a fortune—and I don't mean royalties and that. I mean selected passages: like typing them out and sending them to the people concerned and asking how much it was worth to delete that bit before publication. "Asking"? They could name their price.' He looked grim.

'Are you suggesting Thorne leaked the story himself?' Miss Pink was incredulous.

'No,' Doreen interrupted before Pryce could reply. 'Some other member of the gang, even some other *gang*—yes, that's more likely—' she was excited, '—some criminal in London—could it be the agent after all? He leaked the story, and Thorne took advantage of all the visitors . . . or perhaps he had to steal the book at that moment for some reason. . . . Something had gone wrong with the timing?' She saw Pryce was watching her like an obese hawk and threw up her hands. 'I'm doing your job! I'm so sorry; I got carried away. Over to you, superintendent!'

120

She collapsed with a giggle of embarrassment.

'Gangs.' Pryce tasted it. 'Now that's a nice thought. She was short on brains and Thorne don't seem to have been much cop himself. There's the agent, of course, and who was behind him?' He lumbered to his feet and Williams, like a well-trained collie, left his chair and moved to the door. 'I have to see the forensic people now.' Pryce smiled affably. 'And the pathologist. I'm afraid we'll be busy for a while at the cottage but I'll let you know when we're finished and then you can call in your insurance people. *They'll* be interested in how it started too.'

CHAPTER EIGHT

SAMUEL WAS TAKING in his milk when Miss Pink drove past to her garage. He waved cheerfully as she emerged.

'You're back early! But then you left at some terribly uncivilised hour.'

She hesitated. It was only a matter of time before the police learned that he had been a friend of Sandra. She would warn him. She advanced purposefully and he retreated in surprise into his house. She followed and he closed the door behind her. At the back, outside the open french windows, Caithness was stalking butterflies in the patio.

She gave him the facts quietly but firmly. He dropped rather than sat down. Sweat stood out on his forehead and he rubbed his eye sockets with the heels of his hands as if he could erase the images behind the eyes. After a while he took his hands away and said weakly: 'It's so *wrong!* Both of them . . . burned. . . .'

'I didn't say Thorne was there.' His mouth opened and he gave a shuddering laugh but there was no comprehension in his eyes. 'We didn't see another body,' she went on, 'and

the Spitfire's gone—was gone, last evening.'
She told him about the two visits made by the
television men. His face remained blank. She
stood up. 'I'm going to make some tea.'

She'd switched the kettle on and was looking for milk when he appeared in the kitchen
doorway.

'There's something else; you haven't told
me everything.'

'The book's missing too.'

'What book?'

'Her story; it was kept in the filing cabinet.'

'Oh, the typescript. That's gone? And—
Thorne?' He looked wary. 'I see; he's pinched
the script. His nerve broke.'

The kettle boiled and she made the tea. He
continued: 'Thorne was in a panic yesterday
with the arrival of the reporters. He called
me. What could I say? He wanted to cut and
run but Sandra was for staying on and finish-
ing the book.' He went to put the cosy on the
teapot but his hand was arrested momentarily, then he completed the action. 'So he
drove away and left her drinking in bed?'

'He didn't drive away; the car wasn't outside.'

She repeated the part about the television
men not seeing the Spitfire. For the first time
since she'd dropped the bombshell he looked

her full in the face.

'But that's mad! Why would he hide it, return to the cottage, steal the typescript, then walk away to where he'd hidden the car?'

'I don't know. You say it was a typescript. I didn't see a typewriter.'

They returned to the living room. She looked at the bookshelves, at a door beside the fireplace. It was a long cottage; there was another room on the ground floor which she hadn't seen.

'My study is through there.' His tone was resigned.

'You write too?'

'Comics.' He was belligerent. 'I do the scripts for the pictures: war stuff, flying mostly. Well, it's a living. Naturally—' he was sardonic, 'I expect to write properly one day.' His voice dropped. 'When I have the incentive.' His eyes wandered to the kitten now sprawled panting on the paving stones. He got up and went to move it into the shade but Caithness fastened round his hand like a plush boxing glove. He came back and sat down. The kitten uncurled and studied Miss Pink.

'You were ghosting the book,' she said. 'I thought as much. You were too concerned with it at Roderick's party, and you spent a lot of time at the cottage. She wasn't clever enough to write a book.'

'She couldn't string a sentence together; even her chronology was muddled.' He wasn't looking at her. 'Yes, it was my book, actually—and a lot of good it's done Thorne to steal it; I've still got the notes.' Miss Pink sat up. 'That's how it was done,' he explained, 'And that's why I have to come clean. I made notes there, typed it here at home, and Jakey Jones knew what was happening, so very shortly the police will be calling on me. I suppose it's irrelevant to say that I needed the money.'

'How much?'

'Three thousand. Fifteen hundred down, the balance when it was finished. I'll have lost the second payment but I can't grumble; I've made fifteen hundred in six weeks. Hell! Thinking of the money when she's. . . . I can't bear to think about it.' After a moment he pulled himself together and went on: 'My name wasn't to be associated with it in any way. There's no contract, of course, and no letters, and I was paid in cash; I'm absolved from all responsibility.' He was bitter.

'Are there names in your notes? Real names?'

'No. Don't look at me like that. I really

don't know the names.'

'The police will ask you.' She shifted course. 'Who was her agent?'

'I have no idea of that either. I never met him, I don't even know *his* name. He called himself Julius but by the way Sandra giggled until she got used to it, that was a pseudonym too. I've spoken to him twice on the phone. The first time was when he rang me out of the blue about two months ago. He didn't say how he'd come to hear about me; I guess it would be publishers' talk, or agents. . . . He'd be looking for a third-rate hack who could use a few thousand. He put it to me in general terms: to ghost an autobiography. I said I'd think about it. Within a day or two Sandra turned up—here—and filled in the gaps. I found her captivating and I'm afraid I was amused by the whole project. But the clincher was the money; she had fifteen hundred in cash and you don't argue with a sum like that, and as much again.' He looked at her hopelessly. 'I can't work, you know, with this back; it gives me hell in the winter. But I want—I need to stay here, and where would I go—?'

'All right,' Miss Pink said neutrally, 'you needed the money. I'm not judging you—not for what you did,' she added absently.

'What did I do?'

'Nothing.'

'You don't mean the book had something to do with her death? How could it if it was an accident? You mean, if Thorne had been there, he'd have got her out of the fire?'

'I don't know. Has Julius not been in touch with you since the story broke?'

'No. He hasn't called me since the evening after Sandra came to see me. He rang then and asked for my decision. I never rang him. I don't even know his number. Do you believe that?'

She shrugged. 'The question is: will the police believe you? I think it would be wise to tell them this before Jakey reaches them.'

'It would be more in character for Jakey to come and ask me what it was worth to keep quiet.'

She shook her head. 'He won't have time for mischief. The police will want to see him because he was at the cottage yesterday.' She pondered this. 'I wonder what time he left.'

'He liked Sandra.' He sounded as if he were exploring the statement.

'Did he stay late at the cottage?'

'I was never there in the evenings. In that atmosphere—and in a heatwave, so help me—I had to have some system. We stopped

127

work at tea time.'

'How much did you have to do to finish the book?'

'I reckoned about three chapters.'

'So Thorne would have been in a better position if he'd waited another fortnight, stolen the completed book and your notes as well.'

'Those were to be handed over at the end.'

'Even easier. Why didn't he wait?'

'Because the balloon went up yesterday. The publicity precipitated matters. Thorne felt they had to leave, Sandra wouldn't, so he took the book. Perhaps the idea of that was that she'd follow him.'

'That's far-fetched; all he had to do was to tell her he was going to take the book and the car, and surely she'd be forced to go with him? Or did she have a strong attachment down here?'

'No.' She stiffened and he qualified it reluctantly. 'Girls like Sandra can't afford attachments.' He looked guilty, and perhaps to cover it, asked quickly: 'Do the police know about the leak: who made it?'

'Surely it was the agent: the man you call Julius?'

'That's what Thorne said and I didn't argue with him. But it can't be true; the

128

timing was wrong. You must see that.'

'Well, wrong if there was no ulterior motive.' She stood up. As she moved towards the door, he followed diffidently, the kitten in the crook of his elbow.

'I don't like the sound of that. What kind of ulterior motive?'

'I don't know.' She paused with her hand on the thumb latch. 'And I don't like it either.'

*   *   *

'Just the person we want to see,' Pryce said fruitily as Williams stopped the car on the bridge. He climbed out, wiping his forehead. 'Park on the quay, sergeant.' He surveyed the harbour with satisfaction. 'I've worked in worse places. Does the name George Harte mean anything to you? Harte with an "e"?'

Miss Pink was watching a black-back scavenging on the tide-line. 'George Harte. No, it means nothing to me. What does he do?'

'He is—was Sandra Maitland's agent.'

'Oh.' Her eyes jumped to Samuel's cottage, in full view beyond the green. He said nothing. 'You got an answer to that one quickly.'

'That's how it goes sometimes: a flood of

129

information then, perhaps, a lull.' His face hardened. 'We've had reports on the fire. A couple travelling late pulled their caravan into a lay-by on the main road,' he gestured up the river, 'and they saw the glow a few minutes before midnight. Then a farmer, coming back from town, saw it about ten past twelve. He'd been drinking, the caravanners were strangers; neither reported it until this morning when the news got round about the fire. Started early, didn't it?'

Sergeant Williams had walked back from the quay and stood regarding her with his spaniel eyes.

Miss Pink said slowly: 'She couldn't have been drunk. She was sober at eleven and an hour later the fire must have had a good hold. A glow suggests flames coming through the roof.'

'That cottage,' he said heavily, 'was treated for woodworm last winter, at the same time as it was re-wired. It must have gone up like a tinder-box.'

'She didn't have a chance! But then—'

'Yes, ma'am?'

'Why was she still in bed? You'd expect to find the body under the window—no, there were only skylights. . . . And the floor had collapsed. Even then you'd expect to find a

130

body anywhere *except* on the bed.'

'Did it never occur to you that it might not have been an accident?'

'No.' She stared towards the moored boats but she didn't see them. 'There was a possibility,' she confessed. 'I refused to consider it.'

'But if you had, you'd have thought there were a lot of coincidences, eh?'

'As you do.'

'As we do. A person burned to death in bed is either dead-drunk or—otherwise incapacitated.'

Miss Pink swallowed. 'Dead already?'

'Or unconscious. The post mortem might tell us something; the lungs may be whole. Soot in the air passages will indicate that she died in the fire, but she could have been unconscious when it started.'

'That's vile.'

'I think that too.'

Williams shifted his feet and, catching her eye, nodded agreement. Her face was stony.

'What would be the motive?' she asked. 'He didn't have to kill her in order to steal the book.'

Pryce looked surprised. 'If you reverse that, it makes more sense. From what we've gathered, those two were tensed up from the moment the reporters arrived first thing, yet they didn't have a moment to themselves all day until eleven that night. Then—a quarrel, violence, and him thinking she was dead, and the fire started to cover the crime. On the other hand, it's possible that it's Thorne in the cottage, in which case we're looking for Sandra Maitland. There's only one body. The post mortem will tell us which one it is.'

'How do you explain the car not being outside when the television men arrived last evening?'

'Ah.' His eyes were like chips of rock. 'That's nasty, isn't it? That looks like premeditation. And there's that telephone call to Fleet Street. I've got men looking for people who saw strange cars after dark. The day trippers had gone home but the position's complicated by the reporters' cars. Were they meant to complicate matters? Another coincidence? That someone should ring Fleet Street and get a horde of strangers down here only a few hours before she dies—or someone dies—and a very valuable property's stolen?' His voice changed. 'Thorne could have made that call.'

'Not from the cottage.'

'Why not? The girl was drunk already when she left Mr Bowen's party.'

Beyond the two policemen she saw Samuel approaching across the green.

132

'None of this explains why the Spitfire wasn't outside the cottage late last evening.'

'I've no doubt that will fall into place in good time. Perhaps when we find the agent.'

Samuel had stopped and was looking at the yachts. She frowned. 'You don't think he was down here!'

'He certainly wasn't in his flat. Oh yes, we found that. Not too difficult; *The Sketch* put us on to some publishers who'd seen part of the book: the firm that turned it down. They had Harte's address: a flat in Kensington. Neighbours say he's a middle-aged man who minds his own business. We'll get more in time. He hasn't got a record, not under the name of Harte anyway.'

'You've entered the flat?'

'Not so far. It's under surveillance—'

Williams was signalling to him with his eyes. Samuel had come up and was waiting. Pryce turned and studied him as Miss Pink made the introductions.

'I think,' Samuel said with decision, 'I have to talk to you.' He avoided Miss Pink's eye. 'Perhaps you'd step over to my cottage. You see, I wrote the book.'

CHAPTER NINE

Sparrows were foraging under an open window in Riffli's yard and the sound of sawing came from an outhouse. Norman Kemp looked up as Miss Pink's shadow blocked the light. He was wearing old jeans and a faded fisherman's smock. He straightened his back and gave her a faint smile.

'Good afternoon, Miss Pink?' His voice rose in a question.

'Good afternoon. Is Rachel about?'

'She's gone for a walk.'

'She was going to show me some plants.'

'She must have forgotten.'

'That's not surprising; you've all had a bad shock.'

He nodded miserably. 'How's Roderick? We've not seen him since breakfast time but Doreen rang and gave us the news. How's he taken it? Doreen was rather non-committal.'

'He took it very well, considering. He's not what you'd call fragile.' She smiled.

'Perhaps people can absorb shocks better as they get older. That's more than I can say for myself. But won't you come in?'

134

He moved towards the door and she fell back and glanced round the yard. In one corner was a barn with a flight of stone steps against its gable-end. Raw timber uprights were in position on its outer edge.

He followed her gaze. 'He's definitely not fragile. That's where he took his tumble. I'm putting up a handrail. He hasn't seen it yet. There'll be ructions when he does.'

'Coffee, Norman?' Iris MacNally stood at Riffli's back door, solid and respectable in a tight brown dress. 'It's Miss Pink, isn't it? We were just going to have coffee. Won't you join us?'

'I've come at lunch time.' Miss Pink was apologetic.

'No; we have it early.'

'Local custom,' Norman explained, ushering her indoors and along a stone passage past an open door with a glimpse of slate shelves and huge earthenware crocks.

The kitchen was shaded but hot. On the table flan cases and cakes were cooling on wire trays.

'Baking day,' Iris told her superfluously, clearing a space. 'I should give you coffee in the drawing room but we're all at sixes and sevens today, what with one thing and another. Did Mr Bowen say when he was coming home?'

Miss Pink took off her rucksack and sat down. 'No, he didn't. Have the police been here yet?'

Norman stared at her. Iris said comfortably: 'Not yet. How could we help?'

'About the time of the fire.' Miss Pink glanced at the window. 'You're on high ground. The glow might have been visible from the upper storey.'

'Oh, I don't—' Norman began, and looked at Iris. 'Would we—?'

'It doesn't make any odds.' She took a coffee pot from the side of the stove. 'We didn't see it—at least, I didn't. You couldn't have seen from the yard but I suppose we might have noticed when we went to bed. What time was it?'

Miss Pink accepted a cup of coffee. 'It must have started soon after eleven; the glow was seen just before midnight.'

'Goodness!' Iris reached for Norman's cup. 'Who saw it?'

'A farmer and some visitors.'

Norman shook his head. 'I wouldn't have seen anything from the yard because the outside light was on. I was working late on the handrail. What time did I come in, Iris?'

'It was midnight exactly; I looked at the

time. I was tired and I wanted to lock up.'

'I had to get the uprights in position when the old man was in bed; you know that. And you were watching telly so you weren't waiting for me.'

Miss Pink looked round the kitchen.

'Where were you watching television?'

'In here. I bring my portable down when the others have gone to bed because the sound might keep them awake. Noise carries in this house. Now when did I go up for it? They'd have gone to bed so it would be after ten.

'Perhaps Rachel—?' Norman was curiously diffident.

'No,' Iris said firmly. 'Take a bun, Miss Pink. Rachel would have been asleep as soon as her head touched the pillow.' Her eyes met the man's for an instant. There was a strained silence.

'We—I never got a chance to thank you—' Norman was having difficulty completing his sentences today. 'I mean, you stopped a nasty scene at the party. We appreciate it.' He was stilted, on his dignity.

'Mr Bowen's hospitality was too lavish,' Miss Pink said solemnly. 'And Sandra's entrance came as rather a surprise.'

He looked at her doubtfully. 'I meant Rachel. The point is, she's on tranquillisers,

137

and she's not supposed to mix them with alcohol. It doesn't need much; she had hardly anything that night, I was watching her. But she's never made a scene like that before—'

'Miss Pink doesn't want to hear about our troubles.' Iris was sharp. She went on smoothly: 'There's nothing wrong with Rachel; she's highly strung.'

'You weren't there—'

'I heard about it. I'm sure I'd have been upset if a woman like that walked into my lounge, and it *is* her home, Norman. Mr Bowen should have consulted her before inviting anyone, let alone—well, we all know about Miss Maitland. Actually I'm sorry I missed her; quite a sight, Jones said: diamonds and a white fur! Did you ever!'

'She's dead, Iris.'

The woman put a hand to her mouth. 'There, I was forgetting. Poor thing. I used to smoke but I made a point of never smoking in bed. That's how so many accidents happen.'

'Particularly if you're drunk,' Norman put in.

'We all have problems.' Miss Pink found the housekeeper's platitudes trying but she gave no sign of it. The woman droned on: 'She had no friends down here from what I gather, only the man she was living with, and

138

Jones hadn't a good word to say for him. A lout, he said. Mind you—' she smiled, '—Jones hasn't a good word for anybody except the Lord.' It didn't raise a smile from Norman. 'But I suppose Thorne was a kind of—' She hesitated.

'Pimp is the term,' Norman said, 'with all due respect.'

'As I said: she had her problems. From all accounts she was attractive too.'

'She was beautiful,' Miss Pink said.

'Really? I should have met her. I never ran into either of them.'

When she left, Norman followed Miss Pink into the yard.

'Where are you off to now?' he asked.

'I thought I'd go on the cliffs. I might find Rachel.'

'I hope you do. You mustn't take any notice of Iris; she's a nice old stick but she's a bit dim. She mothers us all, but particularly Rachel.' They were strolling round the corner of the house. 'This path will bring you out to the cliffs. I was saying: Rachel's been a bit uptight lately; she's on these tranquillisers and she does drink with them. The combination has weird effects at times.'

'Such as?'

He was embarrassed. 'Difficult to explain.

She seems miles away: living in a world of her own—I mean, when she's drinking. It's physical, of course, something to do with the effects of the drugs—two drugs—on the brain. To tell you the truth, I'm not sure she's quite with it. . . . It's all right in the daytime, when it's just the tablets, but in the evening she'll have a sherry or two and after a while she gets hazy and then she just flakes out.' He looked harassed. 'And in the morning she can't remember what happened.'

'She must have a reason for taking tranquillisers.'

'It's a combination of circumstances,' he assured her. 'And it's snowballed lately. Rachel always has to be *involved*. She wants to dive in the deep end every time and then she exhausts herself. First there was the nuclear campaign, then we met and we came back here, but the campaign's over and she's got nothing to do. Oh, I know the place is falling down and there's enough to keep me busy for years, but I'm happy to take work as it comes, and the interesting jobs are a man's work. And Rachel can't start slapping paint on windows when the frames are all rotten. She helps Iris, but Iris is quite capable of running the house on her own; she lets Rachel help, like for therapy: knows it does her good if she feels she's indispensable. Trouble is: basically she's superfluous; that's what she says. The idle poor, she calls herself. So she just slopes around the place. . . . That's another thing: she goes out in the dark to watch the Longheads coming out, like badgers. I don't like it. It's morbid. I mean, archaeology's all right but I find all this concentration on the death bit unhealthy. Cracking their victims' skulls to get the brains out and eat them! It's wild!'

'Wrong culture,' Miss Pink murmured.

'I beg your pardon?'

'It does seem a little—perhaps Rachel's something of a late developer; some youngsters do go through a phase of being fascinated by death.'

'If you find her, will you talk with her: try and draw her out? I don't think she tells Doreen much, if anything. Maybe she only tells me. She tells me a lot,' he added gloomily, then his face lightened. 'Iris is a help for all she's so thick. She's reassuring—a bit too much at times. *I* think you should try and face facts.'

★   ★   ★

The Corn cromlech consisted of three upright

slabs supporting a massive capstone. As Miss Pink approached, sheep emerged from the shadowed space beneath and moved away, redolent of hot wool and dung. An abandoned tractor stood in the next field. Despite local custom it would appear that the Pritchards indulged in a protracted lunch hour.

She came to the heath and followed sheep paths through the gorse, not bothering to make a noise for she felt that even an adder would not expose its body to the heat today. All around her the gorse pods were popping in the sun and the strongest smell, above salt and guano, was of scorched grass.

She came to the new fence above the funnel and, crossing it by a rudimentary stile, swung down the miners' track to the top of the great slab.

She stood on the lip and tried to imagine Rachel's feelings as she launched herself out on this sweep of rock (sound but appallingly smooth) with no more security than confidence in her own prowess. Or was it a matter of negative values and Rachel did not know fear?

The slab was empty now and nothing moved in the water a hundred feet below except the dusky forms of the young shag. There was no sign of the old fencing that

Pritchard had tipped down the funnel. It occurred to her that, despite everything, the wire would form a very efficient obstruction to people in boats who might want to approach the cavern, and then she wondered if the tipping had been deliberate: to protect the kittiwake colony. Roderick was a devious old man and the Pritchards an unknown quantity.

She trudged back to the top of the funnel and turned west, arriving in about a quarter of a mile at an empty cottage which she had passed yesterday. Below it was a ravine running down to the sea and there were signs of a path, cropped by sheep and fringed by head-high bracken. Following it downhill she came on the foundations of a number of hut circles. Some of the stones were black and, using a rock as a hammer, she chipped a corner of black stone and underneath it was grey. Did that mean that twentieth century people camped here or that soot could last thousands of years?

Below the site a stream gurgled down steps of boulder clay, its level stretches choked by mint and watercress. A peacock butterfly rested on a stone, grasshoppers clashed like cicadas, and the scent of honeysuckle hung on the heavy air.

The stream slid through a channel where carmine cranesbill made a frieze against the sea. The path swung down to a sandy cove backed by chunky pearl-coloured rock. Off to one side stood a big square stack capped by grass and dotted with herring gulls. Its base was exposed by the receding tide and, crouched in the classic pose of a child above a rock pool, was a figure in a white shirt, but the tawny hair was unmistakable.

Miss Pink looked longingly at the water, jade above the shallows, then took off her rucksack and sat down, wincing at the touch of hot sand. Behind her the bracken slopes rose to an aching blue sky and in front, a chough dropped off the plum-red stack with a piercing 'kee-or!' Rachel glanced up and saw the watcher on the beach. She came wading through the water, her jeans rolled to her knees, her track shoes in one hand, a clutch of shells in the other. Miss Pink beamed at her.

'Is that chough nesting?'

'Yes, they always nest in that place: under the overhang. They've got four young. It's nice to see you.' She was polite rather than enthusiastic. She sat down and placed her shells on the sand. Miss Pink inspected them with interest.

'I looked for you in the other cove,' she

said.

'Wrong place today.' The tone was dreamy. 'Too violent—no; dangerous.' She frowned at her own words. 'The slab needs concentration,' she explained. 'Here, you don't have to bother.'

'Perhaps on a day like this you need to do something that makes demands on you.'

'No. I'm frightened.' Miss Pink turned her head from the sea. 'Of the slab,' the girl went on. 'You can't do something risky when you're thinking about death.'

Miss Pink nodded. 'One has the same feeling after a bad climbing accident. You don't need to witness it; hearing the details is enough. Town councils exploited the reaction when they put wrecked cars at the approaches to towns one Christmas. It slowed drivers down.'

'And they didn't know the people who'd died in the cars.'

'Exactly.'

'I hated her,' Rachel said desolately. 'When she walked in that night I could have killed her. You know that.'

'Primitive feelings.' Miss Pink was equable. 'She was the predator; you were Mum: protecting your family.'

'As simple as that?'

'You can make things as complicated as you like. The problem isn't the *problem*; it's your reaction to it.'

'Say that again.'

'Everyone has similar troubles; situations that precipitate violent emotions: fear, hatred, jealousy. The difference between people is in the manner of their reactions.'

'Wasn't I right to be resentful? It was my drawing room. I was the hostess. She was a threat to—my menfolk.'

'It was perfectly natural. So why are you worried about it?'

'You tell me.'

'Guilt,' Miss Pink said pleasantly. 'That's normal too. It's even there when you lose the person you love most. It passes, but more slowly with sensitive people. I doubt if Norman would feel guilt, for instance.'

Rachel dribbled sand through her fingers.

'Why should he?'

'He was attracted to her.'

'How do you know?'

'No one would be normal who wasn't.'

Rachel sighed. 'Poor Norman. I can feel sorry for him now—now that she's dead. Isn't that ghastly?'

'That depends on how you look at it. You can afford to be generous.'

The girl winced. 'I don't expect he'll meet many ladies as lovely as her again, will he?'

'I don't think it's important. What matters is that you're getting yourself straight.'

'You're so different from Iris! When I talk to her it's like talking to a brick wall: all comfort and clichés; she turns you back on yourself. You tear things apart and put them back again, but differently. I guess Sandra was an ordinary person really, not ordinary exactly, but not all that deviant. I've been thinking about her. She drank a lot and I despised her for it until now, but I expect she was lonely. She didn't have any friends.' She mulled this over. 'Except Samuel.'

Miss Pink hesitated, dismissed the observation that Samuel was a colleague, and said instead. 'She befriended Jakey Jones.'

'Like hell she did!' Rachel was suddenly, refreshingly angry. 'I couldn't forgive that! Jakey's become insufferable over the last few weeks. He told me I was a prude when I said he was too young to go to a—well, you can guess what I called the cottage.'

'How does he manage to get away with his truancy at school?'

'He forges notes from his mother.'

'Boredom,' Miss Pink murmured. 'There's not much constructive activity for a boy like

147

that in Abersaint.'

'It's not boredom; it's his parents. When Grandad's friends come here with kids of Jakey's age, we're always out and we're always late for supper. They're enthralled! They'd love to live down here.'

'What do you do?'

'*You* ask that!' Rachel stared at her in disbelief. 'Why, there's everything. Some of them are as good at flowers and birds as you—well, they're far better than me. And there are the mines, and boats, and the fort—' she smiled engagingly, '—we play Vikings and Longheads instead of cowboys and Indians. That's with the younger ones, of course. The older kids look for arrow heads and dig. Not real digging like archaeologists but we try; we take trowels with us and we spend hours working out how the old people lived. Did you see the huts up there?' She gestured back at the depression in the cliffs. 'They look a muddle, like the fort: piles of stones with the outline of the perimeter wall and just a few circles inside. We try to work it out: what was their design for living. It's fascinating.' She gazed round the cove. 'The Stone Age lasted half a million years.'

'It did?'

'Can you imagine it? Five hundred thousand years and nothing happened. Isn't that lovely? Do you think *they* knew guilt?' She hugged her knees. 'But life did change: they discovered fire and they tamed animals. What must it have been like when the first wolf made friends with the first man? How did the man feel—although it would more likely be a child, wouldn't it?'

Miss Pink said, in the same tone of inquiry: 'Or perhaps a child came on a litter of orphaned cubs and took them home. And the wheel; how did they think of the wheel?'

'Kids playing with round stones, and Dad wanted to move a heavy slab . . . no, dead-end. I know! Boats move more easily on shingle than on sand. Shingle: ball bearings; he'd get the idea when he was dragging his boat up the beach. Why are you looking at me like that?'

'Folk memory,' Miss Pink said. 'Anthropologists talk about the social mind, meaning an amalgam of all our minds. You remember.'

'The stones remember; that's what Avril says. She's the Pritchard girl. She's full of sayings like that. I told her about the Longheads. She said: "You mean them as goes about at night?"'

'Is she afraid of them?'

149

'God, no!'

'Are you?'

Rachel smiled ruefully. 'I've never seen them, not really. Only like now; looking round here—at Ebolion, that's the stack—I know they were here, I know the boats were skins stretched over a frame so they'd be brown, but black against the glare—' she screwed up her eyes, '—you can see them, can't you?'

'Yes,' Miss Pink said, 'I can. You should write.'

'But I don't know anything about them.'

'Bone up on the facts. You're already soaked in the atmosphere. You're like a sponge. Find out what they ate, what they wore, what they believed in, how they buried their dead.'

'Yes, they must have had a religion or they wouldn't have built the cromlech. They were buried with grave goods so that means they believed in an after-life. . . . You may be right. Will you give me a book list?'

'I'll send one when I go home.' Miss Pink stood up. 'I'm going to look at the stream.'

They worked their way up the ravine, water flowing over their feet, Miss Pink calling her companion's attention to each new plant. They explored the hut circles and

150

Rachel insisted that the soot was deposited two thousand years ago. They stood in the garden of the cottage and wondered why rowan trees came to be a guard against witches. The place was leased to a family from Chester who came down for the school holidays.

'It'll be mine one day,' Rachel said, staring at the blind windows. 'I'd rather not.'

'Rather not own it?'

'Not that; when it's mine, it means Grandad will be gone. I inherit the land, you see.'

'I don't think he's worried.' Miss Pink was cheerful.

The girl nodded. 'That's grief, I suppose. They're all right, but you're left behind.'

'Death doesn't matter; it's life that's important.'

They started back along the heath. Rachel sighed. 'And he's had a good life. I know. Not like people being cut off in—' She stopped walking. 'It was an accident, wasn't it?'

'Why do you ask?'

'Because of Tony Thorne. No, don't go on for a moment. I know he's gone. He took the Spitfire.'

'That appears to be what happened.'

'Do you know why he came to the party?'

'To Roderick's party?' Miss Pink's mind raced: the girl's precipitate exit from the drawing room, a slamming door, Thorne's quick arrival, Sandra saying 'he went to the pub'.

'You telephoned him?'

She nodded mutely. They started to walk again.

'Did you make another call that night?' Miss Pink asked.

'No. Why should I?'

'Someone rang the Press after midnight and leaked the story about Sandra's book.'

'I didn't know about the book until the next morning.' After a moment she went on: 'If I had known, and had thought of it, I would have rung them. I'd have hoped it would drive her away.'

Miss Pink was walking slowly, reaching a decision.

'There is something you have to know. The police are not satisfied about the cause of the fire.'

'Mum said she was drinking and smoking in bed!'

'That was the assumption. The police think differently, and they're questioning people: about seeing the fire. It may not have been an accident. With Thorne having

152

disappeared—'

'Tony! You don't mean he—may have killed her?' She stopped and Miss Pink turned to face her.

'The fire probably started before half past eleven. She was sober at eleven, so she couldn't have been drunk when it started. And since she made no attempt to escape, and Thorne has gone—'

'The fire started before half past eleven?'

'It must have done; the glow was seen around midnight.'

Rachel began to walk quickly along the turf. Miss Pink caught her up.

'I thought it better you should hear it from me than from the police.'

'Yes, much better. Thank you.' The tone was absent. 'I didn't see anything. I went to bed early. Norman may have done; he came up a bit later.'

'He saw nothing, but he was working in the yard. Iris was watching television.'

'Oh, you've seen him.' She sounded surprised. 'Yes, the yard's enclosed by the trees; he wouldn't see. . . . But he could have seen something when he came to bed—or wouldn't it have started then?'

'He went to bed after midnight. He couldn't have looked out of the window.'

'Well, I'm glad none of us saw it. A thing like that would be difficult to forget,'—her voice was rising—'and there'd always be the thought that if you'd been quick you might have got over there and pulled her out. But the police think she was murdered and didn't die in the fire. They'll discover that definitely from the post mortem, won't they? I suppose it is her in the cottage and not Thorne? That would put things right: a kind of poetic justice. After all, he exploited her; pimps do exploit prostitutes, don't they? You might say it's an occupational hazard of pimps to be killed by their—what would you call them?—victims. Yes, in this age of women's lib. Tony is the sacrificial lamb. He came to the right place. We had sacrifices too.'

She stopped, gulping deep breaths, her mouth stretched wide, her eyes staring.

'Peking man,' Miss Pink said. The eyes shifted unwillingly, drawn by the sound of the voice. 'Sacrifices and cannibalism belong to a time hundreds of thousands of years ago. Your Longheads were a far more sophisticated culture; in fact, I'm not at all sure that the cannibals were *homo sapiens*, but *homo erectus*.'

'Cannibalism?' Rachel repeated dully.

Miss Pink shrugged. 'Whether or not they

were true man, it was a ritual: in order to partake of your enemy's courage.' She took the girl's arm and drew her gently along the path. A sheltered dell opened at their feet and the baby rabbits went scampering into their holes. Rachel's eyes followed them.

'And surely,' Miss Pink went on slyly, 'only a vegetarian can condemn cannibalism.'

'People are human!'

This was a well-worn channel to Miss Pink, one where she could steer Rachel clear of dangerous shoals, and which would keep them going as far as Riffli. But whereas the argument was now concerned with man the carnivore versus man the vegetarian, with dentition, nutrition, and the percentage of plant foods in the diet of the Kalahari Bushman, on a different plane of consciousness Miss Pink was wondering about the results of the post mortem and, as a corollary: the identity of the body in the mill cottage.

CHAPTER TEN

SOMETHING MOVED IN the grass in one corner
of the graveyard and Samuel started to stalk
it with a wild hope in his eye. A jackdaw got
up, squawking. Did jackdaws eat carrion? He
lurched forward and tripped over a fallen
tombstone.

'Caithness,' he cried, picking himself up.
'Caithness, are you *there*?'

He trampled the grass where the bird had
been, his head sunk between his shoulders.

'Have you lost your little kitty then?'

He turned slowly. Jakey Jones was leaning
against the wall of the church. He lifted a
king-size cigarette to his modelled lips and
exhaled through his nostrils.

'It might not be dead,' he said pleasantly,
turning the cigarette and regarding the glow-
ing end. 'He could be dying—very slowly—
right now.'

Samuel's arms hung loose. He didn't look
in the least angry, indeed, he too was smiling.
He took a step forward.

Miss Pink unlatched the graveyard gate
and tramped up the pebble path.

'I want a word with you,' she said to Jakey,

156

ignoring Samuel, 'before the police get to you.'

The boy stiffened. 'They've gone.'

'They'll be back.'

'My kitten's missing,' Samuel said, his smile a rictus. 'He's got it.'

'That's most unlikely.' She held Jakey's eye. 'He's got too much on his mind right now.' She beamed at the boy who wasn't smiling any longer. There was silence from Samuel. She saw that the boy's hand had moved surreptitiously behind his back and was in view again, without the cigarette. Jakey's face was devoid of expression and the curiously blank eyes, without impudence or fear, moved to the gate, the back of Samuel's house, the hotel across the water.

'They will be back,' she repeated. 'Come to my cottage.'

'I'm not going nowhere with you.'

She nodded. 'Quite right: to remember what your father told you. Never go anywhere with strangers; there's no knowing what they might have in their handbags, even old ladies: hypodermics, poisoned sweets,'— her eyes dropped absently to his heels, '—pot.'

'What he's afraid of,' came Samuel's voice from behind her, 'is abduction. His mother

157

told him what happens to small boys.'

'Male prostitution,' Miss Pink said kindly. 'Or modelling for blue films. I suggest we go and sit on the wall in full view of people on the beach where you know no harm can come to you, and have a little talk.'

There was no need. Samuel was making for his cottage, leaving her a clear field.

'So.' She became business-like. 'Officially you were the handy-man for Miss Maitland. You washed the car and cut the grass; what else did you do?'

He started to grin. 'Is them the questions the police will ask?'

'Are they aware of your part in it yet?' He gasped and swallowed. 'Were you paid hourly or by the week?'

His head had dropped, now it came up and he squinted at her like a stage villain. 'I got a pound an hour.' She opened her mouth but he hadn't finished. 'Sometimes she give me a fiver.'

'Indeed. I will not ask you what for. How did you manage to fix it with your parents?'

'I didn't have to!'

She shook her head reprovingly. 'Oh come; you're not telling me they were aware of your real relationship with her.'

'They didn't even know I was up there.

158

They thought I were on the beach, or some-where.'

'They knew you weren't at school?'

'They're not going to know. I took me mam's notes.'

'Forged.'

'What d'you think?'

'You have a most unusual life ahead of you.'

His chin went up and his nostrils flared. His hand moved to the pocket of his jeans.

'Do smoke,' she cooed.

He lit up with fascinating nonchalance, watching her through the smoke.

'Were you never resentful of other men?' she asked.

A look of uncertainty crossed his face. 'Why should I be? Jealous, d'you mean? *Na*, it was her job.' He sneered. 'She passed the cash on to me, didn't she? Tax free.'

'Thorne had to be paid too.'

'There was enough for all of us. She was big-time.' He drew luxuriously on the ciga-rette. It was obvious that although he con-sidered they had some mutual interest in perfidy, he thought she could still be impressed—and to judge from her interest, she was.

'She wanted me to go back to London with

her,' he resumed carelessly.

'Would you have liked that?'

'You have to be joking! After this dump! It's all happening in London. And New York. I might go on to New York.'

'When are you leaving?' The tone was courteous, not inquisitive.

He inhaled again. 'Soon. Quite soon.'

'And who is going to sponsor you?'

'Come again.'

'Who are you going to touch for the money? Are you sure you have the right person, because if you made a mistake—'

But he'd shrunk away. The cigarette lay smoking on the ground. Lifting his feet carefully he walked down the path, not fast but tense as an animal that knows it's lost if it breaks into a run. She stubbed out the cigarette and straightened, watching him pass through the gate. He threw her one last look and vanished beyond the wall, reminding her of a collie slinking out of a lambing field with blood on its jaws.

Samuel must have been watching from his house. He came climbing over his patio wall and strode through the grass.

'You don't think he's got him?'

'What? Who?'

'Caithness.' He was almost beside himself.

160

'He got over the wall; I thought he wasn't big enough. I missed him only half an hour ago. Did that little bugger say anything?'

Miss Pink looked into the imploring eyes. 'No, I don't think he's got Caithness. Why don't you look on the beach? He might be with people down there.'

'Oh, yes!' He started to plunge away. 'What were you talking about?' It was an afterthought.

'Nothing to interest you at the moment. You look for your kitten.'

As soon as she set foot in the hotel, Miss Pink was aware of a difference in the atmosphere from last night. The receptionist, immaculate in silver eye shadow and not a hair out of place, greeted her from behind her desk, and her expression was merely welcoming. From the direction of the bar came a subdued murmur of conversation. There was none of the excitement of last evening; there were no reporters. Things were back to normal, except for Rupert—or did he normally eye his guests warily as he greeted them? Could he still be feeling his way into the role of mine host?

A stranger stood at the bar whom he introduced as Mr Carter. She saw a small, hollow-eyed man with a thin mouth and a fleshy

161

nose. There were deep lines between nose and mouth. His hair receded, his cheeks were sunken, and his lightweight fawn suit had been made for a plumper man, or for this one before he lost weight. He looked like a sad comedian.

'Miss Pink,' Rupert was saying, 'is a great bird watcher.'

'A pleasant pastime,' Carter observed. 'Quiet and peaceful.'

She thought of the fierce sea cliffs, and Rupert caught her hesitation.

'Not where *our* birds are concerned,' he put in. 'You've got to be a mountaineer to get into position to watch the auks.'

'Auks?'

Rupert deferred politely to the expert.

'Guillemots and razorbills,' she told him. 'Like penguins. You're quiet tonight.' She looked meaningly at Rupert. She didn't want to disturb his guests unnecessarily, but she need not have worried.

'I was discussing it with Mr Carter. The focus has shifted to London. The post mortem's over and the forensic people have about finished at the cottage so they're concentrating on looking for Thorne. I understand the police are still interviewing reporters who were at the cottage yesterday but they've left the village. They know all about the fire now.'

'I don't,' Miss Pink said. 'I've not heard anything. Do you know the result of the post mortem?'

'No surprises. She died in the fire.'

'It was her then?'

He looked puzzled. 'Of course it was. And there's a brandy bottle near the bed, a melted ash tray and a lighter, damaged but identifiable. I identified it, as a matter of fact.'

She said nothing, and realised that they were both watching her.

'No surprises,' he repeated.

'Have the police found the Spitfire?'

'Not to my knowledge. They may never find it. Stolen cars can disappear without trace.'

'Any word of the agent?'

'I wouldn't think so, or it would have leaked through. The police rang about the post mortem because it's our business in a sense, but we're not concerned with who did it.'

'"Who did it"?' Carter repeated slowly. 'I thought you were implying it was an accident.'

Now Rupert was the focus of attention. He was flustered.

163

'Who took the Spitfire, I mean—and the book. The book was stolen.' It sounded weak. He glanced at Miss Pink as if for assistance. 'You were up at Riffli,' he said meaningly. 'Norman came down and told us.'

Carter said quietly: 'A girl's dead and her fellow's missing. Do I take it that the police suspect foul play?' His eyes rested on Miss Pink.

'Oh, I don't think so,' Rupert rushed in. 'She drank heavily, and the lighter being there points to. . . . And then she couldn't get out; there was no window.'

'A bedroom with no window?' Carter looked interested.

'Only a skylight,' Rupert said. 'And if the door stuck—she was overcome too quickly anyway; she was lying on the bed—' He stopped and glared at Miss Pink.

'How is your father?' she asked, a little too loudly.

'Oh, Roderick. Yes, he'd like a word with you. Upstairs. Something about—er—insurance? If you'll come with me, I'll take you up to him.'

Doreen was with Roderick in the sitting room. Miss Pink sank down beside the old man on the white settee.

'Find Rachel?' he barked.

Rupert, on his way to the door, paused. Doreen looked tense.

'Yes,' Miss Pink said. 'She was in the cove on the west shore, where there's a stack called Ebolion. We had a long talk.'

'What about?'

'Dad!' Doreen looked shocked. 'Don't pump Miss Pink.'

Rupert took a step back into the room. 'Can I get you a drink?' he asked hopefully.

'You'd better go back to the bar, sweetie,' Doreen said. 'I'll see to the drinks.'

Rupert hesitated, shrugged and went out. Doreen sat down near the window, her back to the light.

'I'm glad you met Rachel.' Her tone was brittle. 'Did you swim? That cove's lovely for swimming.'

'No.' She was aware of Roderick's scrutiny. 'We talked about pre-history: the fort, hut circles, how the people lived. She has a most fertile imagination. I think she could write.'

'Do yer, by Jove!'

'You don't think she's just a little too im-aginative?' Doreen was all maternal anxiety.

'No.' Miss Pink returned the other's gaze. 'She's dramatic but there she takes after Roderick. I don't know where the line comes between imagination and fantasy. When she

165

can manipulate her thought processes, control them, channel them, with some competence at syntax she could make a novelist. The potential's there.'

'Good!' Roderick exploded, slapping his knees. 'Great—as she'd say.'

'I think control is the operative word,' Doreen said. 'She's a passionate child. Always has been.'

'Sudden fierce spurts,' Miss Pink qualified. 'They're soon over.'

'You discovered a lot in one talk.'

'It was deliberate; I wanted to get to know her. She's an interesting study.'

Momentarily Doreen's face lost its brittle quality and she gave Miss Pink a grateful smile. In this transformation there could have been an element of relief.

'What d'yer mean: I'm dramatic?' Roderick growled, but there was an impish light in his eyes.

'The branch on the granary steps.'

She'd confused him. He blinked and averted his eyes, then he muttered: 'Made a mistake; must have got so absorbed in me owls, I didn't hear it come down.'

Miss Pink stared at him.

Doreen said conversationally. 'As you'll have noticed, we've got rid of the police—and the Press, thank goodness; they took up a lot of room in the bar—the Press, I mean, not the police. I understand they've all pushed off to London, after Thorne, although that wouldn't be ethical, would it? Pryce would have to sub-contract to the Metropolitan people.' She gave her tinkling laugh. 'But you'll know far more about police procedure than we do. Pryce will have to pay us one more visit though; he has to see Jakey Jones.'

'Couldn't he find him today?'

'He went to school—and that's not to be wondered at. On an occasion like this young Jakey would put as great a distance as possible between himself and the police. He's got too much to hide. He can run rings round our local bobby, but a detective superintendent is a very different kettle of fish.'

'What time does he go to school?' Miss Pink asked.

'The school bus picks him and Ossie up about eight-thirty from the green. Why?'

'No one knew about the fire until after nine: when the television men went to the cottage. How would Jakey know the police were coming?'

'Coincidence,' Doreen said.

*   *   *

Miss Pink ate her solitary dinner and slipped out of the hotel without meeting any of the Bowens again. It had been a long day.

The sun had set and against the luminous sky the swifts were hawking through the dusk with thin high screams of excitement. A shadow moved among the shadows of the fish sheds: disappearing, reappearing in another place. He came softly and lightly across the cobbles and bent to peer under the first parked car.

'Samuel! Haven't you found him yet? Come back to my place and join me in a night-cap. I'm feeling a bit low.'

'You are? Why?'

'Reaction. At this time last night she was still alive.'

It was crude but at least he turned and started walking with her. She was prompted less by compassion than by the fear of his running into the execrable Jakey, who knew so well how to exploit human frailty.

The fish sheds muffled the sound of the engine until the last moment and it was a shock when the yellow Mini came slewing and roaring off the Riffli track, tyres screaming, and the little car slid crab-wise before it settled facing them and they heard the crunch of bad gear changes.

'Christ!' Samuel gasped. 'That's Norman! For Heaven's sake!'

The Mini leaped towards them. They stepped back hurriedly to give it a clear run to the hotel but it stopped, the driver's door flew open and Rachel ran towards them.

'Sam!'

He put his arms round her. 'Take your time, kid. You're all right; I'm here. . . . What's wrong?'

She pushed back her hair. She was shaking and she was a bad colour. Between broken breaths she jerked out: 'It's Iris . . . dead . . . on the table. . . . The poker. . . . I can't take it; I can't take any more, Sam, honest I can't. She's all covered with burns, naked. . . . The poker's in the fire.' She buried her face in his chest.

'She's hysterical,' he said.

'Shocked,' Miss Pink corrected, 'but not in hysterics.' She glanced towards the Mini, its engine still running. Rachel lifted her head.

'We have to go back!' She broke away and ran to the car. 'Quick,' she shouted, 'she may not be dead.' She started to turn the car.

'Whatever's happening?'

'Let's go and see.'

They piled into the back of the Mini, Miss

Pink bracing herself against the front seat but, surprisingly, Rachel drove slowly at first, along the quay and up the track. Samuel was leaning forward, grimacing with tension as he studied her profile.

'What *is* it, love?'

'I told you: Iris is naked on the kitchen table covered with burns and the poker's in the fire. The door of the Aga's open and the end of the poker's sticking out. Someone's burned her.'

'Who else is there?' Miss Pink asked.

The car leaped forward, crashing over the cattle grid. Miss Pink and Samuel were thrown back in their seats and then flung sideways as they bucketed round the bend. The trees rushed to meet them.

The yard showed ahead and Miss Pink's abdominal muscles contracted.

Rachel stopped, facing the kitchen. The light was on, the casements open. From their low seats they could see nothing more than the beamed ceiling, the top of two walls and an empty clothes rack. Rachel sat still.

'Go and look through the window.' Her voice was terrible.

They got out and approached the window and stopped. They looked from the bare scrubbed table to the Aga with its fire door closed, the empty clothes rack, the gleaming sink. Miss Pink walked back to the Mini.

'There's nothing on the table,' she said.

Rachel stared through the windscreen. Samuel approached and looked at Miss Pink.

'She's been moved,' the girl said tonelessly. 'Dragged down to the cellar, or put in the freezer—if there's room.' She studied their faces which were intent but kind. 'Yes,' she said, 'I have to go right to the bottom now, don't I?'

Miss Pink flinched. Rachel got out of the car and led the way indoors. It was a warm evening in the open but the heat of the house struck them like a blow. They went along the stone passage to the door of the dairy which was closed. Rachel opened it, switched on a light, went to the freezer behind the door, turned to Miss Pink as if to ask a question, then sighed deeply. She lifted the lid. Samuel and Miss Pink looked blankly at the packages which more than half filled it. Rachel closed the lid without looking at them and walked out.

They followed her to the kitchen. She crossed to a door beside the fireplace and opened it, clicked another switch and illuminated a flight of steps. They descended and walked round the cellar among wine racks and old grain bins. The lighting was excellent. There were no dim corners and nothing untoward, not even rats.

They climbed the steps and put out the light and shut the door. They had said nothing since Rachel left the car and now, standing by the cooker, clasping her elbows and shivering in the stifling atmosphere, the girl said: 'We have to search the house.'

'Very well,' Miss Pink began, but at that point they all heard footsteps on the stairs. Samuel put his arm round Rachel.

High heels clacked along the passage and a voice said: 'I thought I heard the car—why, good evening!'

Iris MacNally, in her old brown dress, came in carrying a vase of wilting roses and crossed to the sink. Miss Pink was just in time to help Samuel as Rachel crumpled to the floor in a dead faint.

CHAPTER ELEVEN

MISS PINK AWOKE with a sense of doom and lay staring at the drawn curtains recalling her conversation with Rachel yesterday. Had something she'd said precipitated that ghastly hallucination? For that was what she thought it was. When the girl had been carried upstairs to the room she shared with her husband, the bed was made, the counterpane uncreased. If she'd had a nightmare, she hadn't been sleeping here, although that was what they'd told Norman when he appeared on the landing as they struggled up the stairs: that Rachel had had a nightmare.

Samuel and Miss Pink had come down to the kitchen as a car drove into the yard. Doors slammed, there was a flurry in the passage and Doreen whirled in.

'What happened? Rupert said Rachel tore down to the quay like a mad thing and you two piled in . . . Well, what *has* happened?'

Roderick stumped in after her, looking pathetically tired.

'She had a horrible dream,' Miss Pink said. 'A nightmare.'

'So what?' Doreen snapped. 'She wasn't

alone up here, was she?'

'Iris heard her drive away. She thought she was upset about something. Norman was around.'

'When?' He appeared behind them in the doorway. He sighed. 'Hello Doreen, Rod; they've told you then. Iris is with her now. She's come round.' He slumped into a chair.

'Had you been quarrelling with her?' Doreen asked viciously.

'What? When she passed out? I haven't seen her all evening—yes, I have; I went in the drawing room about—Christ!' He dropped his head in his hands. 'Oh, nine-ish, I guess. She was in there then.'

'What was she doing?' Doreen asked.

'Drinking,' he said resignedly.

★   ★   ★

Miss Pink got out of bed and parted her curtains. The sea was bland and beautiful and her spirits rose a little. All problems were capable of solution. Perhaps Rachel's youth would make the solution easier, or easier to find. Nevertheless she had no doubt that the problem was neither tranquillisers nor alcohol; they were merely symptoms.

She swam before breakfast: working hard,

174

concentrating on her rhythm and, as she turned for the shore and waded out, two gulls came swooping along the edge of the water, screaming and diving.

She stood dripping, her shoulders heaving, and peered at the flapping birds. On the wet sand a tiny black and white object checked, ran, crouched at a gull's steep plunge and she heard, above the wash of low waves, a spitting hiss. She lunged forward, whirling her arms.

'Get off, you bastards!'

Caithness scuttled to her and crept, quivering, on to her feet. She knelt and he jumped on her thighs. He was boned like a robin, too small to fondle. Where has he *been?* As she rose he fastened his claws in her swimsuit and clung like a burr. She walked back to her wrap, the kitten immobile and silent in a wide-eyed trance.

The french window was open on the patio. She called to Samuel from the graveyard side of the wall, handed Caithness over and went away quickly, leaving him to croon over the prodigal.

It was late when she finished breakfast. She went down to the quay and mingled with the first visitors emerging from their cars. The vehicles were being marshalled by Caradoc Jones, a man of many parts, now authoritative with a leather satchel slung across his chest.

Miss Pink found herself beside him and remarked that the village was returning to normal with the police and the Press departed, and, for herself, she was not sorry to see them go. All the same, she added with a fussy air of trying not to give offence, it would have been good for trade.

'We can do without that kind of custom,' he told her loftily. 'I was in Lord Barmouth's service at one time; he would have thrown reporters off the estate.'

Miss Pink said that she supposed they were only doing their job, but that unfortunately they did attract undesirable elements.

'I had my hands full yesterday,' he confided, 'and we haven't seen the last of them. Someone asked me just this minute where was the cottage and whether the body was still there.'

'But they could be useful,' she mused. 'A lot of people roaming the countryside: inquisitive, poking in odd corners, dogs off the lead in the woods; they might find a clue—like the Spitfire—' her eyes were round behind her thick spectacles, her voice awed, as if at her own temerity, '—even Thorne's body.'

He regarded her with condescension.

'You've been misinformed, madam; Thorne drove away in the Spitfire and is now being sought in London.'

'Jakey's a very bright boy.'

Caradoc had hazel eyes which protruded slightly and now, as he turned on her, rims of white showed round the irises.

'You know where he is?' he breathed.

'Is he not at school?'

'Oh yes, he's gone back to school.' It emerged like a disclaimer to something in his mind. His mouth twitched. A car hooted, traffic was snarling on the quay; he disregarded it.

'My boy has not been himself lately,' he said with care. 'Mrs Jones kept him home while he was sick but he went back to school yesterday. He's a very bright boy, tries hard—too hard; he's studying for his O-levels but they say he's over-taxing his brain.' He sought for something better. 'He's subject to stress.'

'It must be very difficult to keep an active boy indoors when he's off school.'

'We do all we can.' His eyes went to the traffic jam, returned to her apprehensively. 'We both work for Mr Roderick, at least the wife works mornings. We can't be at home all the time.' He started to edge away.

'What time did he come home Wednesday evening?'

He wiped his palms on his trousers. 'Wednesday evening?'

'He was at the mill cottage.'

'Oh no.' He shook his head vehemently. 'No, he wasn't.'

'I saw him there.'

Caradoc drew himself up, his face wet with sweat. 'You were mistaken, madam; my boy never went near that place.

* * *

The Jones's cottage was on a knoll and approached from the green by one of the sunken alleys, this one slipping through the gap between the back gardens of the Post Office and its neighbours.

It was a white cottage with a primary blue trim, its front garden walled with stone finished by horizontal slabs so highly polished that they resembled marble without the streaks. Dotting the baked earth of a flower bed were stiff isolated specimens of marigold, lobelia and a pink snap-dragon. It was a bright tidy unhappy garden. A slatted metal mud trap guarded the slab outside the open front door. Miss Pink wondered if the slab

178

could be black-leaded. It shone like ebony.

The room inside the door was dim beyond the sunlight but there were gleams from pale furniture which was covered with china ornaments and brasswork. There was a smell of Air Wick and fried meat.

The mud trap rattled under her feet and there was a sound inside like rats disturbed. Thirza Jones came to the door, blinking in the sunlight.

'It's Miss Pink,' she said unnecessarily.

'You're not well, Mrs Jones.'

The woman's eyes were bloodshot and the fingers that traced the line of her lips trembled uncontrollably. Miss Pink had come with questions but in the face of the other's obvious distress she could not ask them, or perhaps, she thought with a sinking heart, they were already answered, but she had to say something; she couldn't turn away in silence.

'I've been talking to your husband, Mrs Jones; I called to ask how you were.'

Thirza stared listlessly at her. A bumble bee was caught in the bell of a snap-dragon, buzzing in a panic of claustrophobia.

'My boy hasn't done nothing wrong.' It sounded like an incantation, as if she had said it many times before.

179

Miss Pink said; 'Jakey's young, and Mr Pryce is an understanding man. Where is Jakey now?'

Thirza's eyes were focused on something beyond the fish quay. 'Who's Mr Pryce?' she asked dully.

'Superintendent Pryce.'

The woman's face was flooded with hostility.

'They've got no call to come here! They wants to go to that Myfanwy Post: ask her what her boy was doing when my lad were tucked up safe in bed. Sending a patrol car after him! Parked on the green for all to see. It's not right! We're decent people, not criminals.'

'Last night?'

'Last night. Parked on the green—' she was working herself up, '—but Jakey'd gone for a walk—' She stopped and twisted her hands. 'I've got the milk boiling over,' she said wildly. The door slammed in Miss Pink's face.

She retraced her steps down the steep path. Through the gap between the houses she saw a familiar black car slowing to halt on the green. On her left an alley branched off, twisting round a corner. She took it and, stopping beyond a straggling dog-rose, leaned

180

idly against the wall. After a moment Pryce appeared, followed by Williams. They climbed the bank to the Jones's cottage in silence and she heard the mud trap rattle under their feet. She turned away and continued along the path which ran into that which debouched beside her own garage. She let herself into Captain's Cottage and went through to the terrace where she sat down and leaned back in her chair. Her thoughts were almost unbearable.

A footfall alerted her. Samuel was stepping over the wall from the graveyard, Caithness peeping coyly from inside his shirt. She looked at the two faces, both ingenuous.

'Well,' she said with assumed cheerfulness, 'that's one problem solved.'

Samuel said feelingly: 'I wish I could have the opportunity to save your life.'

'Nonsense. He was holding his own very well against the gulls.' She told him about the birds and he shuddered.

'That's one crime that can't be attributed to Jakey Jones,' she said grimly.

'Little sod! I'd have throttled him if you hadn't come along at that moment.' He looked murderous, then his face changed, became acutely anxious. 'That was a bad business last night.'

'How is Rachel this morning?'

'She's better; at least, she's gone out.'

'On her own?'

'Yes. I don't like it. Neither do they. I spoke to Norman on the phone. He's worried out of his mind. I—I'm very fond of Rachel, in an avuncular fashion.'

'She turned to you in an emergency.'

'I wish the emergencies weren't there that she had to turn to me. They should get her to a doctor, not let her go out on her own, but she's stubborn as a mule. What's behind this?'

'Sandra's death?' Miss Pink wondered. 'Fire was the common factor: burns.'

'Poor kid.' He was anguished.

'I talked to her yesterday, I thought she was very reasonable, at first.'

'Then?'

'Sandra's death again; she's worried about that. Samuel, the police are at Jakey's house; they're looking for him.'

'Now? I saw the car on the green last night.'

'They missed him. I've just seen Thirza Jones. Pryce is with her now.'

'What are they after?'

'You asked me what Jakey said last evening: when I told you to go and look for Caithness. Something odd happened; he was

182

boasting about the life of crime that was opening out for him in London and New York—'

'What!'

'Thorne's influence, I suspect. But his reaction was peculiar when I asked who would sponsor him. He didn't understand so I asked whom he would touch for the money. That frightened him.'

'Is that when he slunk away?'

'That's right.'

'*Touch* for the money? Did you mean some kind of blackmail?'

'I didn't. It appears that he thought I did.'

The doorbell rang. When she opened the door she was so surprised that for one moment she couldn't put a name to the caller: the lined face, the intense eyes. . . .

*　　　*　　　*

'Mr Carter! Good morning.'

'May I come in?'

She hesitated, then led him to the terrace, murmuring politely about the weather, wondering what on earth he could want with her. She introduced Samuel. Carter studied the other man carefully, his eyes resting for a moment on the kitten, still opting for safety inside the shirt.

'We know each other,' he said.

'Good God!' Samuel sat down heavily. Miss Pink stared at Carter.

'He's Julius,' Samuel said weakly. 'I recognise the voice.'

Miss Pink closed her eyes in an effort of recall. 'George Harte?' she asked coldly.

'Carter,' he corrected. 'Harte is a trade name.'

'Sit down, Mr Carter,' she was stern. 'Why have you come here?'

'I came to Abersaint because I have an interest in what happened here. I came to you because you know it wasn't an accident, and I'd like to hear more about that.'

'The police know it too. You realise that I shall inform the superintendent in charge that you're here.'

'That doesn't bother me; I've done nothing illegal. But you may not want to go to them after you've heard what I have to say.'

'No? And what's your side of the story?'

'My *story*. It's enlightening.'

Caithness emerged delicately from Samuel's shirt, dropped to the ground, walked over and leaped on Carter's lap. He didn't touch the kitten but he smiled an extraordinary sweet smile. 'It's Thorne's story

184

really,' he said. 'I was on my way home from Italy early yesterday morning and I arrived to find the papers full of Sandra and her book. So I didn't go to my flat but to another place, and it was there that Thorne rang me and told me what had happened. What he had to say brought me down here. And don't ask me where Thorne is. I don't know.' He paused but they made no comment. He went on: 'Thorne didn't go to the door with the tele-vision men. He had no indication that any-thing was wrong until after they'd gone, when the police rang and asked if he'd lost a car. He says the local men would know the Spitfire. He looked outside and saw it had gone. He went upstairs and Sandra—who was already in bed—said she left the car out front with the keys in the ignition. She was like that.

'Thorne gave the copper the registration number and the fellow said it was in a field— the last on the left before you come to the main road. He said one of the tyres was flat; otherwise it was undamaged and the key was in the ignition. He suggested that Thorne should come and collect it, and he rang off.

'Thorne went back upstairs and had a quick word with Sandra. They agreed that the Spitfire had most likely been taken after dark and probably when several other people were driving away. They thought it might have been taken about ten-thirty and they reckoned it was this lad, Jakey Jones, who'd gone for a joy-ride. Incidentally, Sandra was very tired and cold sober; my first thought was that she'd had a terrible accident with a cigarette and drink, but Thorne said she wasn't drinking, nor even smoking, and there was nothing on the bedside table but a clock. I got the picture of a very tired girl wanting only to go to sleep.'

The lines in Carter's face seemed to have deepened. Absently, with a gentle finger, he started to rub the angle of the kitten's jaw. 'So,' he continued, 'Thorne set out to walk up the valley. The car was in the field all right, and with a flat tyre. There was no sign of the police. He pumped up the tyre and drove back to the cottage. When he got back it was blazing. He didn't stand a chance of getting in. So he came south and got in touch with me. He said there was nothing wrong with the tyre he'd had to pump up; it had been let down deliberately: to keep him away from the cottage that much longer, just to make sure she'd die.'

In the sudden silence they could hear Caithness purring happily. Miss Pink didn't stop to analyse why she should find this sound slightly shocking. Her mind, perhaps in self-defence, caught on a trivial point.

'Sandra said her name was part of the disguise, and Cynthia Gale was how she was known in London. Why do you call her Sandra?'

'That *was* her name. Cynthia Gale was how she was known professionally. It doesn't matter.'

'No. Where is the proof for this story?'

'There isn't any—unless I produce Thorne, which I can't, but you'll know whether it fits the facts.'

'The suggestion is that the murderer hid the Spitfire in order to get Thorne away from the cottage?'

'There was another objective. At first it was thought to be an accident, but if the police saw through that, Thorne was in a position to be the prime suspect.'

'Why should you believe him?' Samuel asked.

'If he'd been the killer he wouldn't have phoned me. Besides, he had no motive.'

'The typescript,' Miss Pink put in.

'He didn't steal it; he couldn't enter the cottage.'

'That's working on the premise that part of his story is true. He could have killed her and taken the script, set fire to the cottage, then given you a story that was totally fabricated.'

'He's still got to sell the book to some kind of agent. He had an agent—in me.'

'If blackmail rather than publication were the object,' she pointed out, 'he wouldn't need any help for that.'

Carter didn't turn a hair. 'He would. Thorne was a small operator—and he knew his limitations. And he knew Honey had the notes; that's proof that the book is ours, if he wanted to sell it elsewhere.' He looked at Samuel. 'I shall want those notes.'

'The police have them.'

They regarded each other like two strange dogs.

'Why aren't you going to the police with this story?' Miss Pink asked.

'They wouldn't believe me.'

She stood up and walked to the graveyard wall. The kitten yawned and stretched, jumped down and lay in the shade of the fuchsia hedge. Miss Pink came back and sat in her chair.

'Now tell us why you've come to me.'

'The killer's a local man. Do you have ideas about that?'

'No.' It was too quick.

'There was a telephone call to Fleet Street.' He looked along the terrace. 'At twelve-thirty on Tuesday night.' He glanced at Samuel. 'Who made it?'

The other was wary. 'We assumed you did.'

'Thorne may have assumed that. You wouldn't, nor this lady. Who knew she was writing the book, besides yourself?'

Samuel's head moved fractionally but he didn't look at Miss Pink.

'What makes you think it's a local person?' she asked.

'Because the man who claimed he was a policeman told Thorne exactly where to find the Spitfire. The business at the cottage looks like two people: one to take the car, the other to kill the girl and set fire to the place. There'd be signals between them so that one could let the other know when the reporters were safely away from the cottage. That could be done with a torch. So who knew about the book besides yourselves?'

There was a pause. Miss Pink said: 'I didn't know.'

'So only Honey knew.'

Samuel said firmly: 'I didn't call Fleet Street. It would be cutting my own throat—financially.'

'It would,' Carter agreed.

The doorbell rang again. Alarm flashed between Miss Pink and Samuel, and was

189

observed by Carter.

'Will you answer it?' he asked politely. 'If it's the police, I don't want to talk to them yet, and I think you ought not to until we've finished this discussion.'

She stalked through the sitting room and opened the front door.

Caradoc Jones stood on the step and he was furiously angry. He pushed past her and walked into the room where he wheeled and confronted her.

'You brought the police!'

Miss Pink took a breath and noticed out of the corner of her eye that her other visitors were invisible beyond the open window.

'He's being victimised!' Caradoc shouted. 'Mrs Jones is collapsed! She suffers with her nerves.' She tried to speak but he rushed on: 'He's got a right to go where he likes! Not illegal, is it, to go *walking?* Boys is boys; whatever he's done, it's all the fault of that Ossie Hughes. Corrupting influence, that's what he is; my boy's been under my eye all the time—' His mouth hung open as Carter appeared in the doorway leading to the kitchen. 'Who're you?' he yelped.

Carter looked him over carefully. 'What time did Jakey get home Thursday: very early, just after midnight, after the fire started? Half an hour? An hour?'

Caradoc's hands went to his throat in a gesture that was effeminate yet poignant. 'He never—' He could get no further.

'Did you see him come in?' Carter was implacable. The other shook his head dumbly. 'He comes through the window then.' Caradoc stared like a petrified rabbit. Carter took him by the arm. 'Come on; I want a word with your boy.'

Caradoc jerked free. 'He's not at home.'

'Ah no; he'll be at school.'

'He's not then!' It was an echo of Jakey. 'There's no school today. They've got no water.'

'So where is he?'

There was a gleam of defiance in the other man's eye as he drew himself up. 'I don't keep track of my son's whereabouts.'

'Except midnight Wednesday, or early Thursday, when you know he wasn't in bed.'

Jones gulped and blundered out of the room. Miss Pink took a step towards the door but he was letting himself out. Samuel appeared in the kitchen, Caithness on his shoulder.

Carter said: 'Jakey was at the party during the evening, serving drinks. Thorne doesn't remember seeing him after ten-thirty, and he

191

had a good look because he didn't like having the boy around. He'd caught him playing Peeping Tom once. Unfortunately Sandra was inclined to make a pet of him; like befriending a rattlesnake, Thorne said. Are you going to the police Miss Pink?' The tone was insinuating.

She looked at him without expression. Silence hung between them.

'Motive,' he said thoughtfully. 'Someone killed her to get the typescript? A local person was mentioned in it?'

'For God's sake!' Samuel exclaimed. 'I wrote the thing; no local people were mentioned.'

'Do you know the intimate history of all your locals? Actually, Thorne bears you out. Sandra never so much as hinted that she'd known anybody down here previously. There were men—' his eyes narrowed, '—but no one serious. Thorne would have known that too.' The others were tense. 'No,' he went on, as if one of them had spoken, 'she wasn't having an affair with a local. This was a premeditated crime; not a violent sex quarrel.' Miss Pink saw a flaw but her face was schooled. 'Although,' he continued, as if telepathic, 'if someone thought she was having an affair with a husband or boy friend. . . . a woman

192

will go to great lengths to kill carefully, methodically . . . then you could have a premeditated crime. What was wrong with Rachel Bowen last night when she carried you off in such a hurry?'

Samuel gasped.

'She'd been drinking,' Miss Pink said.

'She wasn't that bad.' Samuel's voice sounded strange. 'There was an Alsatian loose in the woods and she wanted help to catch it before it got among the sheep.'

They waited, bristling, for the next thrust. Etiquette was a thing you took for granted until it was torn to shreds like a spider's web ripped by a bull. Miss Pink stood in her own house and was afraid to show him the door. He was more than clever; he appeared to know what she was thinking. Now he said quietly:

'I won't trouble you any longer; I'm not in a hurry and I've got nothing to lose.'

They both knew it was a threat. Neither of them moved. He walked to the door, then turned. His head was lowered slightly and in the dim corner his eyes gleamed.

'She was beautiful,' he said. 'And helpless.'

The door closed quietly behind him.

CHAPTER TWELVE

SAMUEL WAS THE first to speak.

'Do you believe it?'

Miss Pink roused herself. 'As Carter says: it fits the facts—but so would a fabricated story if a clever man made it up.' She removed her spectacles and massaged the bridge of her nose. 'We might do some checking; the last field on the left before the main road, he said. You take the kitten home; I'll get the car out.'

Within a few minutes they were driving round the green, slowing to a crawl as they encountered a gaggle of small children trailing towards the beach and licking ice creams.

'There's Ossie Hughes on the bridge,' Samuel said.

She stopped the car. 'He may know something. Act casually; see if you can draw him out.'

They strolled towards the bridge exchanging chat about the basin. '. . . Would hold far more boats if we could get it dredged,' Samuel was saying. 'Morning, Ossie. No school then?'

'No water at school.' Ossie squinted against the sun. ' 'Cos of the drought, innit.'

'Huh.' Samuel's face appeared to mirror

the other's: the jaw slack, the eyes bored. 'Going swimming?'

'No one to swim with.'

'It was bound to happen eventually; he's got tired of you trailing after him all the time and he's gone off on his own.'

'It weren't like that!' Ossie was near to tears. 'Me mam wouldn't let me go, would she? No good asking her even.'

'Chicken,' jeered Samuel. 'Jakey wouldn't ask his mam; he'd walk out.' Ossie shrugged mutely. 'When's he coming back? I've got a job for him.'

The boy was startled. 'Jakey'd never work for you!'

Miss Pink put in her oar. 'I've been talking to his parents; I forgot to ask for an address. He's given you one, of course?'

'Address?'

'For writing letters.' Samuel mimed scribbling on his palm.

'Yeah, I know,'—indignantly, '—he didn't give me no address.'

'It will be the same as Tony Thorne's.' Miss Pink tossed this casually to Samuel but Ossie's face was blank.

'Why didn't he go with Thorne instead of following him?' Samuel asked in a tone that echoed Miss Pink's indifference.

'What's it got to do with Tony?' Ossie was bewildered.

'He has to join a gang,'—Samuel became patronising—'he doesn't know any of the big names, like the Krays and the Richardsons. Hell, man, he doesn't even own a shooter!'

Miss Pink decided he'd over-played it but as she turned to stroll back to the car, Ossie said stoutly: 'He will then! He said as he'd get a shooter—*and* a Mini, he said: a brand-new one, not like Kemp's old banger—' He checked and, with a fine disregard for priorities, muttered: 'That's Mr Kemp up at the big house.'

Before Samuel could comment on this, Miss Pink asked inquisitively: 'Why *didn't* you go with him? He could have used you. He was talking to me last night. After London: New York, he said. You'd have made a good lieutenant.'

Ossie blinked and dropped his head. His fingers worked a piece of mortar out of a cranny and he hurled it in the stream. 'He didn't ask me.'

She sighed sympathetically. 'So all you could do was see him off, pretending you didn't really mind—'

'Didn't know he'd gone till I got up!' He brushed his eyes with the back of his hand and glowered at her.

'Didn't he tell you last night that he was going?'

'I never saw him after tea. Me mam called me in and he went over to the church. *You* was there.' He turned accusing eyes on Samuel.

'Who told you he was gone?' Miss Pink asked, but the boy merely stared at her.

'He's not gone,' Samuel sneered. 'You're making it up! He's hiding somewhere. You're in it too. He's not run away at all.'

'He has then! His mam came down to our place before breakfast. He didn't come in last night and she said as how he were out wi' me. I didn't even know he'd gone! Why d'you all think *I* know where he is?' His lip protruded. 'He said he were going to London but he didn't say when. He's gone, ain't he?'

'There's the money angle,' Miss Pink said meaningly to Samuel, who nodded.

'Who gave him the money?' he asked roughly.

'What money?'

'The train fare—the shooter, the new Mini: all the bread he was going to get. Who'd he get it from?'

Ossie looked blank. 'I dunno.'

'When did he tell you about the money?'

Miss Pink asked.

'Before tea time yesterday: here on the bridge.'

'Why didn't he tell you during school?'

'I dunno. I didn't see much of him. He were quiet, funny like: he didn't talk to me till we got home.'

'What kind of guy is that: can go up to another guy and ask for—' Samuel rolled his eyes, '—over two thousand quid, with the Mini?'

This was too much for Ossie. An expression of acute helplessness made him look like an idiot. 'He allus talked like that; I didn't take no notice.'

'What use would a Mini be to him anyway?' Miss Pink was disgruntled. 'He can't drive.'

'He can then! He drove *her* car.'

'Pull the other one.' Samuel was bored.

'He did! He use ter drive to the road-end and back again. She taught him.'

'Was he a good driver?' Miss Pink asked.

Ossie blossomed at the opportunity to answer a question without having to think about it. 'He were fabulous! It were all going for Jakey!'

★   ★   ★

'Did you notice,' Samuel observed as they drove up the valley, 'that he used the past tense most of the time?'

'Yes . . . but he's not intelligent. If Jakey's left the village, Ossie might think of him as having gone away for good, hence the past tense.'

'So soon? It looks black for Jakey. Still,' he added grimly, 'if they start with animals, they'll go on to people eventually. A psychopath—not a budding one: he's fully-fledged, at fourteen!'

'He came into my mind when Roderick said someone deliberately placed a branch at the top of the granary steps.'

'You thought of Jakey then? Before anything happened at the mill?'

'Roderick said there'd been an attempt on his life. Jakey was the only person I'd met or heard of who might fit the bill; in fact, he fitted very well after I'd seen him roll a boulder down the cliff on—' she hesitated, '—nesting kittiwakes. There have been killers of his age before now; as you say, they start with animals.'

'There have been rumours about cats,' Samuel said tightly. 'That's why I reacted like I did yesterday. And he'd be aware that I knew of the rumours so his taunts were the essence of sadism—'

'Where's the gate?'

'It's round the next bend; there it is. Slow down. . . . Why are you going past?'

'Tracks. We'll park on the main road.'

A hundred yards west of the Abersaint signpost was a large lay-by and a telephone kiosk.

'Telephone handy,' Miss Pink observed, getting out of the car. 'Would you think that Jakey could imitate the voice of a man? A young man, say.'

'The call that lured Thorne away from the cottage—if Carter's speaking the truth. It strains credibility. I've used disguised telephone voices in my comics but I've no idea whether it can be done in practice.'

They walked back to the road-end and down the lane. 'Dry as a bone,' she observed, studying the grass verge outside the gate. 'There are tracks here but they could have been made by tourists' cars.'

The gate was fastened by a rusty cow chain. Its timber was by no means new but it opened in one piece, enough to allow the passage of a car. On the farther side there was a brackeny shelf before the paddock dropped steeply to the river in its belt of alders. The bracken had been lightly crushed by wheels and the tracks were fresh.

'It fits,' Samuel said.

Miss Pink stared absently at the crop of foxgloves in the hedge. She said slowly: 'My mind had been running on the theory of Jakey's having seen the killer and blackmailing him, but if Jakey drove the car—and killed the girl—why would he be touching anyone for money? What would he have to sell?'

'The typescript. He's taken it to London to find a buyer.'

'He's not clever enough to make a deal like that.'

'He's pathologically conceited.'

'There is that,' but she sounded dubious. 'If he rang Thorne, posing as a policeman, from the kiosk in the lay-by, how long would it take him to reach the cottage from here—but across the fields? He couldn't run down the lane because Thorn would be coming up it. Thorne would never go across the fields in the dark; he wouldn't know the way.'

'It's roughly two miles across the fields, about the same distance as by the road. He couldn't do it in less than half an hour, with all the banks to climb over in the dark. There's no path.'

She led the way out of the field and he fastened the gate. As they strolled up the lane she said: 'I'd like to get a look at the lie of the land. We don't have to go high—' she was looking at a sloping field beyond the signpost, on the other side of the main road.

'You can't see the cottage from here; it's hidden in its dell; didn't you notice when you were there? It was its main attraction: the privacy.'

But Miss Pink was determined and Samuel had to toil up slippery grass behind her in his Hush Puppies. However, she stopped after a couple of hundred feet and they sat down and surveyed the view.

To the south-east stretched the patchwork plateau of small irregular fields broken, in the middle distance, by the valley of the millstream: a caterpillar of woodland with a blue bloom on the foliage from the heat haze.

'Is it really two miles?' she asked.

'A mile and a half perhaps; it's still going to take a while to run it in the dark.'

Back at the car she got out her large-scale map and studied it.

'I'm going to look for Rachel,' she said. 'Will you run me to Corn and take the car back to the village?'

He bristled with suspicion. 'Why do you
202

want to see her alone? And how do you know where she is?' She regarded him speculatively and the hostility faded from his face. He said simply: 'I'd do anything for Rachel; you see: I love her.' He bit his lip and scuffed in the gravel with the toe of his nice shoe.

Miss Pink was suddenly galvanised into activity. 'Right. Let's go to the headland, and we'll go by way of Corn so that we don't attract any unwelcome hangers-on in the village.'

'Like Carter?'

'Carter, Pryce, anyone.'

★   ★   ★

They stood at the top of the funnel. Nothing moved in the searing heat: not even a gull showed above the lip of the cliffs.

Miss Pink said: 'You don't like steep ground, do you?'

'I wouldn't be here if it wasn't for Rachel.' He couldn't face the funnel squarely and was squinting down it from the corner of his eye.

She left him sitting on a rock on the level heath and, promising not to be long, she descended to the top of the slab.

The tide was ebbing and the exposed barnacles were a wet brown fringe at the edge of the navy sea. The cliff plunged, first the colour of claret, then black, straight into the cove and the water was flat as the surface of a pond. A huge jelly fish drifted in the shadows. The shag were not out today but occasionally a kittiwake dropped from the roof of the hidden cavern and flew languidly out to sea. There was no sign of people.

She retreated to the miners' track then traversed into the shaft, skirting the awful drop. A bat flew out of the depths and jinked away in the sunshine, then she heard the singing.

It came from the shaft: pulsating and familiar. It was blowflies. Pritchard had lost a sheep. She hoped it wasn't alive.

She climbed the funnel to the old mine level above the scree tip. It was forty feet deep, Rachel had said. The roof was just a little too low for her to walk upright and she had to proceed in a kind of half crouch. She penetrated a few yards then waited against the wall, allowing the light to show her the next stretch and her eyes to get used to the dimness. The floor of the tunnel was flat and firm but scattered with small spiky stones. There was mud in the interstices and the tracks of little cloven hoofs. The walls dripped. There was no sign of a human footprint.

She reckoned she'd gone thirty feet when

the level changed direction slightly but enough to ensure that the rest of it was dark although points caught the light: a streak of wet rock, a puddle, odd unidentifiable things. She didn't think there could be a hole in the floor and since there was no level below, the ground could not give way suddenly—which was always a possibility in old Cornish tin mines, but an atavistic fear of the dark and of falling forced her to go down on all-fours and edge forward, carefully sweeping the ground with her hand.

It was very dark. She turned her head and saw the empty passage, the walls bulging against the secondary light beyond the bend, and she saw something move.

She held her breath, feeling a stone under the palm of her hand, clutching it. The thing moved again. It was water dripping, catching the light against a shadowed crack.

She exhaled, turned slowly and extended her hand. It touched hair.

She shrank back against the wall. There was no sound except, at long intervals, a drop falling from the roof into a puddle. 'Rachel?' she breathed. No sound.

She edged forward and groped: the feel of hair at her fingers' ends before she touched it, and so she realised now that it was very coarse hair, frizzy hair—it was wool.

She prodded it in an excess of relief. The sheep didn't move. Her hand felt over the fleece to the leg, but it wasn't a leg; it was a bone—as it would be. If it had been an animal that had died recently, like the one in the shaft, she wouldn't have got this far for the smell—at least, not without *knowing*. If the one in the shaft wasn't smelling, that meant it was very recent indeed.

She felt round the walls of a little bulbous chamber that marked the end of the level. Her feet scrunched among skulls. She wondered why they'd died.

'Where did you go?' Samuel asked curiously on her return.

'Exploring an old level.'

'No sign of her?'

'Only sheeps' skeletons.' She started for the stile. 'Rachel gets on well with the Pritchard girl, doesn't she? Let's go and have a word with them.'

The Pritchards were still hay-making. As Samuel and Miss Pink approached the man switched off the tractor and got down to the ground. Two collies came streaking towards the walkers, their bellies low, but at some signal and without checking their speed, they curved away to the bank where they dropped in the shadows. Their movements were fast, neat and totally silent. Miss Pink was reminded of hunting dogs trained to run soundlessly. She regarded the Pritchards with interest.

The man and his daughter were short and heavy but Mrs Pritchard was a slight middle-aged person with smudged grey eyes, sparse hair and a cigarette dangling from the corner of her thin mouth. Avril Pritchard was a pudding of a girl in a dipping brown skirt and black pullover, her bare feet thrust into laced walking shoes crusted with dung.

Mrs Pritchard took the cigarette out of her mouth revealing, not the hard face of a slattern, but an expression full of amiable curiosity. Samuel was introducing them.

'Like a smoke?' Mrs Pritchard asked affably.

The visitors demurred. 'It's very hot,' Samuel protested. 'We—er—were thinking of having a swim.'

'You come past Pentref,' Avril said.

'Pentref?' Miss Pink glanced at Samuel.

'You shoulda swum there,' Avril pointed out, 'where the old people live.'

No one corrected her tense. Miss Pink sought for an innocuous topic. 'You've lost a sheep in the old mine shaft, Mr Pritchard.'

'There are no sheeps in the mines.' Mrs Pritchard was smug. 'That's why we put the new fence up: to keep 'em inside. You saw an old body.'

'I saw nothing. How could I? There are flies in the bottom of the shaft.'

'Bones sing,' Avril said, and giggled.

'We're looking for Rachel,' Samuel told her firmly, like a school teacher.

'Everyone's looking for someone today.' The girl grinned and scratched her thigh. 'There's Norman and you after Rachel, and the other one after Jakey Jones.'

'What other one?'

'Him what's sick.'

Samuel glanced at Miss Pink for help; he wasn't so much at home with the Pritchards as with Ossie Hughes. Thinking of Pryce's paunch, she said: 'The police don't get enough fresh air and exercise.'

'Was he police?' Mrs Pritchard asked of Avril.

Miss Pink asked: 'Did he have lines here—' she traced lines from her nostrils to the corners of her mouth, 'and was he very thin and rather sad?'

Avril nodded. 'He'd lost something. He was after Jakey Jones but we don't know where he is so we couldn't help. And we can't help you neither: 'bout Rachel.'

The Pritchards were suddenly embarrassed and avoided each other's eyes. A curlew wailed in the next pasture. Miss Pink studied the slopes of Carn Goch thoughtfully.

'Perhaps she's on the mountain. Are there holes on the mountain?'

'Foxes' holes,' Pritchard said.

'She couldn't hide in a fox's hole.'

Mrs Pritchard was lighting a fresh cigarette. 'She don't need to—'

Avril made a movement. 'No one'll find her; not till she's ready.'

Her father turned to the tractor. Miss Pink said urgently: 'We could help; we're her friends. . . .'

Samuel looked at Avril imploringly. 'She trusts me. Is she at Pentref? It was closed when we came past.'

'She's not there. Leave her be.'

'So you know where she is.' He was desperate. 'Is she at Corn?'

'We ain't seen her today.'

The tractor fired. Miss Pink said: 'Will you tell her I want to see her: anywhere she likes? Tell her we're on her side.'

'We got to get on with the hay.' Mrs Pritchard moved after the tractor. Avril went to follow then looked back. 'After dark. She won't come in the daylight.'

'Why ever not?' Samuel shouted.

'It's safer in the dark.'

'Is it to do with Jakey?' Miss Pink called, but she was speaking to their backs.

Samuel said quietly: 'They know where she is. Who's she hiding from?'

'Pryce? But he's looking for Jakey, not for Rachel.'

They started to walk towards Corn where they'd left the car in the farmyard. Samuel glanced behind. 'What is it? Is there some link between that little monster and Rachel? Could she be protecting him?'

Miss Pink said: 'I wonder whether she'll come down to the village tonight. We've got a long time to wait until dark. . . . Samuel! Can you get hold of a boat—not in the village, Pryce might be there. Can you get one from this side of the peninsula, so that we can approach the headland without the whole village knowing?'

'There's Parry Lobsters at Cae Coch; he'd lend me his boat. Why?'

'I think I know where Rachel is.'

'That's what you said about the mines. A boat? You think she's in a cave? Could be. I must go back and feed Caithness first; it won't take ten minutes from the road-end.'

It took longer than he'd anticipated. Miss Pink parked on the green and went to her own cottage for her swimsuit. In her bedroom she glanced out of the window and her attention was caught by the sight of a man, fully-dressed, wading in the shallows. A uniformed policeman watched him from the water's edge.

She went out on the terrace and parted the fuchsia twigs. Pryce and Williams were talking to a group of visitors on the shore. Others were clustered at a discreet distance with the selfconscious but eager air of eavesdroppers. She took the key of her bottom gate and went down the flight of steps in the corner of the terrace.

'. . . don't usually,' Pryce was saying, 'but it was a warm night. Ah, Miss Pink. Good afternoon, ma'am.' He drew her aside. 'You've heard?'

'No; I've been out. I've just come back.'

'Let's walk down to the sea; some of these have ears like bats. We found his clothes.' She stared at him. 'Jakey Jones,' he elaborated. 'There were jeans and a pair of track shoes down here, no shirt or shorts; we're looking for those—but he could have been wearing swimming trunks. A family back there found them. They came down at eleven

211

this morning and the things were there then, just below high-water mark. There were people swimming so they didn't take any notice until the tide came in and then they got worried because no one had claimed the things in two hours. So they took them up to the Post Office and the boy there identified them. He's Jakey's pal.'

'Ossie!'

'That's right: Ossie Hughes. Gave him a nasty shock. I've been talking to him. The clothes have frightened him.'

She was bewildered. 'You think Jakey drowned?'

He shrugged. 'It happened just below your cottage, ma'am. He didn't come home last night. Did you hear anyone on the beach after dark? Or see anything?'

'No; I'd had a hard day and went straight to bed when I came in.'

He looked interested. 'Visiting, were you?'

'I have my dinner at the hotel. How do you know that Jakey wasn't home last night?'

'Ossie Hughes told me. The Joneses aren't saying anything, but I've not seen them since the clothes were found. I'll have to go and talk to them again now. Unpleasant job. Ossie said Jakey was with you at tea time yesterday. Honey too. When would that be?'

'About five o'clock. I met him in the churchyard.'

'What was he doing there?'

'Having a quiet smoke. I shouldn't be surprised if he were also waiting to see if Mr Honey would leave his windows open and go away; he was looking for his kitten.'

'Like that, was it? What did you talk about?'

'He told me something of himself. He used to do odd jobs at the mill cottage and had inflated ideas concerning his future. He talked about going to London.'

'So Ossie said. Did he say anything else?'

She thought about this. 'He said Sandra Maitland paid him well.'

'Indeed. The reporters say that he was there the evening that she was killed.'

'She *was* killed then? Rupert Bowen said that she died in the fire.'

'Who set the fire? And there's nothing to say she wasn't hit first. The brandy bottle found near the bedspring was Martell Cognac; that comes with a long neck, not flask-shaped. Handy weapon. A bruise wouldn't show—now.' They had halted on the damp sand. The man in plain clothes was still wading in the shallows, and the uniformed man paced the water-line, a sur-realistic figure in the flat bright bay. Pryce turned and looked back at the shore.

'What are his clothes doing here?' he asked quietly. 'Would a young lad go swimming alone at night? There were people about all evening; he couldn't have got into difficulties without someone seeing in the daylight.' He shook his head at the sea. 'I don't think he's out there.' Miss Pink said nothing. 'Ossie,' Pryce went on, 'is convinced he's gone to London but that could be a defence mechanism because the clothes still frighten him. He's not a very bright lad. Well, what about this Jakey: has he followed Thorne?' He cocked an eye at her. 'Did he see something on the night of the fire?'

'You're suggesting he left the clothes on the beach as a blind?'

'Been done before, hasn't it? Plenty of times. So far, ma'am, you appear to be the last person to have seen him before he— disappeared. The dreaded punch-line!' He chuckled. 'Any advance on five o'clock?'

'I've no idea where he went after he left me—'

He wasn't listening. Following his gaze she saw Caradoc and Thirza Jones coming across the sand, the woman in a bright pink overall.

214

They walked side by side without touching or talking and they stared stonily ahead as they tramped over the wet sand.

They stopped. Thirza's eyes were empty but in Caradoc's there was a dull black panic. Thirza addressed Pryce.

'Who did it?'

'Why wasn't it an accident, Mrs Jones?'

'It was an accident,' Caradoc intoned.

Miss Pink was anguished and she ignored Pryce. 'Mrs Jones,' she said sensibly, 'it might not be what it looks like; it could be—'

Thirza said, her voice riding over the other's: 'Who took him in the water?' She stepped up to Pryce, her face twisted with hatred: '*You* know.'

He said firmly: 'I know no more than you do; less perhaps.'

'We don't know nothing,' Caradoc said in that terrible monotone.

His wife turned and stared beyond the village. 'He was there that night.' Her voice was hollow. 'He saw it.'

'What did he see, Mrs Jones?' Pryce was gentle.

She plucked at the loose skin of her throat as if she were trying to get rid of it. '*She* had to die, ' she said with sudden helplessness. 'If it wasn't then, it had to be sometime soon. But it had nothing to do with my boy. He hadn't done nothing.' She looked at her husband piteously. 'He shouldn't have been out so late. We never liked him being out late, did we?'

Pryce took her elbow, motioning Caradoc to take the other. 'We'll go home now, Mrs Jones—'

She snatched her arm away. 'I'm going to look for my boy!'

'Leave it to the police,' Caradoc said wildly, trying to get hold of her wrist. She threw him a glance of agony.

'But can they find him in time?' She turned to Pryce. 'What have they done to him?'

Miss Pink recalled Samuel's anguish as he searched for his kitten. 'I'll help, Mrs Jones; everyone will help. . . .' Help look for a monster? She felt tired; even monsters have mothers. Thirza ignored her anyway; limp as a drugged doll, she was being led away by the two men.

CHAPTER THIRTEEN

'Let's get this clear,' Samuel said, 'Thirza and Caradoc think he's in danger—right?'

'Perhaps worse,' Miss Pink said absently, slowing at the junction with the main road.

'But why? I can understand you and Pryce assuming that Jakey'd got himself into trouble he couldn't get out of this time, but the parents—at least, most parents—would go on hoping till the last. Why does Thirza assume the worst?'

'Subconscious?' she mused. 'All her life she's fought for him, blocked out his anti-social behaviour. . . . I don't expect they ever discussed him between themselves: Thirza and Caradoc. Now she's exhausted; for years she's known it would come eventually: something too big for him to wriggle out of. Retribution, she'd call it, if she's Chapel, and blame herself. She's doing that already.'

'So *you* think he's dead too.'

'I was trying to interpret Thirza's thought processes.'

She helped herself to a sandwich from the box on his knee. They were eating as they travelled, having given less attention to their stomachs today than to the kitten's, and now she had been forced to telephone the hotel to say she wouldn't be in to dinner. She had spoken to the receptionist which was just as well; the Bowens would have asked questions.

'Do you think he's dead?' Samuel repeated.

When she answered, her mind had jumped a few stages. 'Almost as if we've reversed their roles,' she murmured, 'as we learn more. First, I thought of Jakey as a spectator: someone who saw too much and tried to cash in on what he'd seen. But the Spitfire business suggests he's a participant. But since Rachel is hiding something—and appears to be hiding herself—one wonders if she was the spectator. That's why we have to find her, and why I'd like to know what's happened to Jakey. If he dumped his own clothing as a blind, he could be anywhere now—' she glanced towards the sea on their left, '—one thing: he can't get to her without a boat.'

'You think he's dangerous—to her?'

'That depends on his part in the murder, and on what she knows—but I feel sure those two are connected in some way.'

'And always remembering there were two killers, because the fire started so soon after the telephone call—the one that was supposed to come from the police.'

Miss Pink, who'd been pulling out to pass a bus, swerved back and threw him a startled glance. She drove on in silence, not noticing the smoke belching from the bus's exhaust.

'Cae Coch coming up,' Samuel said. 'Turn left here.'

It was low tide. The bay on this side of the peninsula was immense and the few people left at the end of the day were lost on vast stretches of opalescent sand.

Parry Lobsters lived close to the sea: a small man like an ineffectual ferret, with a squint and a cloth cap. His boat was high on the shore. Miss Pink had forgotten the state of the tide but by means of a trailer and a number of male tourists who emerged surprisingly from Parry's cottage, they manhandled it to the sea. The owner seemed to be enjoying a private joke, one eye on Samuel trying to start the outboard, the other on the horizon, but when they'd got going, chugging towards the headland, Samuel pointed and she saw that, westward, the horizon ran straight into a belt of fog.

'Can you manage?' she shouted.

He pursed his lips. 'It may not be travelling fast. How long do you want to spend with her—if we find her?'

'If she'll answer my questions, ten minutes

would be enough. We could do it in less if she'd come back with us but there I think we may have trouble.'

'We'll manage. I can crawl along under the cliffs—and we can swim.' He grinned.

For the first half mile the coast was rock at an easy angle: the chunky pearly rock that extended to the cove below the hut circles. The cove was less romantic this evening: flat and green in the late sunlight, with the square stack indistinguishable from the land. At the top of the ravine the cottage faced blindly out to sea, the sun reflected in its windows. The hut circles looked like nothing more than scree in the lush bracken.

After Pentref the cliffs increased in height and angle very quickly. The tilt was diagonal and from the foot of every buttress long reefs slanted into the sea. The rock was jet black below but dusted with golden lichen above the reach of the spray and streaked with emerald where freshwater springs came down. There were caves under stupendous overhangs and the water inside them, even near the ebb, appeared fathomless in the gloom. Nothing showed in the backs of the caves, only now and again a cormorant crossed their wake and rose to a hidden ledge.

There was a scattering of razorbills in

pockets but no guillemots because they like horizontal ledges and there was none. Despite that Miss Pink could trace lines on the rock by means of which a hard climber might explore this wild waste of virgin rock, but he would have to be good.

She became aware that Samuel was asking no questions. True, it would be difficult to communicate above the noise of the engine, and impossible without shouting, but he showed no interest in the cliffs. Then she realised that he was watching the fog bank.

He swung out to clear a reef of gaunt triangles. Glancing over the side as they heeled, she saw a long thick shape slip through the oar weed. 'Conger!' she shouted. Samuel grimaced.

They rounded the end of the reef and the funnel presented itself dramatically, appearing vertical but with the zig-zags of the miners' track marked by its turfy parapet. The cavern gaped below, light reflected on the walls and dipping roof. Now she could see that there were jutting corners inside and on the left piled boulders gleamed wetly, indicating a rockfall. The shag were swimming under the roof and when Samuel closed the throttle, the clamour of the gulls rose above the soft chuckle of the engine.

'There's wire here,' he said.

'It'll be close to the cavern, where it fell. Take me in to that shelf at the foot of the slab.'

He peered at the cavern. 'She's here?' he asked incredulously.

'She could be; I've seen her come down this slab.'

'Good God! Does anyone else know?'

'I hope not. Put me ashore; we haven't long before dark.'

'What about me?'

'You drop anchor and wait.'

He looked stubborn. 'If she's here I want to talk to her.'

'That's sentiment; I *need* to talk to her: to ask some questions, but I'll try to get her to come back with us.'

'But surely I'm—'

'No.' She was firm. 'You're not objective. Let me start the ball rolling.'

They'd drifted to the foot of the slab and she stepped out on the rock shelf.

'Hand me those plimsolls.'

He passed her a pair of track shoes and watched morosely as she stripped, revealing powerful thighs and still more powerful shoulders, and a thick tanned torso clad in a regulation swimsuit. She took off her boots and put on the track shoes.

'You've still got your specs on.'

'I need those.'

'But—the wire.'

'If she does it, then I can.'

She walked along the shelf until the rock came down and barred further progress. Across the water the young shag collected like ducks and paddled along the foot of the cliff. She lowered herself into the sea, wincing not so much at the temperature but the ambiance. It was not the kind of place one would choose for a swim.

Keeping as close to the rock as possible, cringing from the weed that slyly stroked her skin, she dog-paddled towards the great portal. Hundreds of eyes watched her from the roof and on the shadowy walls the shags' necks swayed like serpents. Cold with apprehension, her eyes wide behind her spectacles, she drifted into the cavern and something moaned.

It rose and fell and echoed, resonant in the rock, and it was absolutely ghastly. It stopped. So had she, her feet dropping to tread water, feeling sick from the embrace of the weed.

The sound came again: swelling, dying, inhuman but only a shade off human; it was the similarity that made it so dreadful. She looked back and saw Samuel staring towards her. She was aware of the water lapping her neck like fingers that in another moment would close on her larynx. With a feeling of ineffable sadness—the feeling that verges on the ultimate fear—she lifted her eyes reluctantly from the surface of the water in time to see forms dropping from the roof. She ducked, choked on salt, whirled with a great splashing, pawed her eyes, and saw the rock pigeons, silhouetted against the light, veering to avoid the boat.

Now the kittiwakes discussed her presence among themselves but without panic and she knew that she was on the right track. They were accustomed to swimmers in the cavern.

'Where are you?' she called loudly. 'Don't keep me waiting; I've cut myself on the wire.'

There was a movement in a recess, too extensive for a bird. 'Oh no! I'm here: where you're looking.'

A corner protruded, seaward of the rockfall. Miss Pink gave a couple of broad strokes and touched submerged rock.

'Watch your feet,' came Rachel's disembodied voice. 'Feel you way over the blocks—but the cracks go deep.'

She lurched over immense and slimy angles

to emerge dripping on a wet ledge.

'Crawl up,' came the instructions. 'Feel for the holds.'

'This is the limit!' She slipped and struck her knee cap. Pain shot up the nerve to her hip.

'Are you badly hurt? Should it be stitched?'

She continued crawling in a disgruntled silence and her questing fingers discovered a curious texture, like quilting. 'How on earth did you get a sleeping bag here?'

'In a plastic bag. Where are you hurt?'

'I'm not; it was a ploy to get you to speak.'

'I thought as much,' the girl said composedly, 'but I couldn't risk not answering. You might have bled to death in the water and then it would have been my fault.'

Miss Pink could just make out a pallor that must be her face. They were in a dark corner facing the back of the cavern. Leaning out she could see Samuel hunched in the boat.

'Are you warm enough?' Rachel asked.

'I'm all right; I won't be here long.' Despite herself she sounded as if she were on the defensive.

'What's happening in the village?'

Now Miss Pink, who had been trying to discern the other's expression, blessed the darkness which hid her own.

'The police are still looking for Thorne, but in London, and the Spitfire hasn't been found.' Rachel made no comment. 'She did die in the fire,' Miss Pink said gently. 'She wasn't killed first.'

'She was unconscious.' The tone seemed to imitate that of Miss Pink. 'She didn't feel anything.'

'How was she rendered unconscious?'

A long pause. 'With a heavy candlestick.'

'Odd,' Miss Pink mused. 'Why not a bottle?'

The atmosphere was heavy with tension.

'It wasn't a premeditated murder,' Rachel said. 'Things just happened; there was no choice of weapon. It was the first thing that came to hand.'

'Why did it have to happen at all?'

'Rage.' There was a sharp exhalation that could have been a kind of laugh. 'And that wasn't intended either. At first it was to be a confrontation: keep away from my family or else. . . . But you know—you saw her poise; even lying in bed she had poise. I was trembling when I went up the stairs. . . .'

'What did she say?'

'She seemed surprised. I told her to lay off. She said she'd never had anything to do with Norman. She laughed at me. I hit her.'

'How many times?'

'Once. It was a heavy candlestick—pewter; did I say that already? I didn't mean to hit so hard. Do they all say that? But I thought I'd killed her so I had to set the place on fire to cover up.'

'How did you do that?'

'Just brandy: spilled on the bed I'd rather not talk about it if you don't mind.'

'What time did you set the place on fire?'

'I can't remember.'

'When did you get back to Riffli?'

'I don't know that either but it would be around midnight.'

'Did you have a car?'

'Of course not. I went and came back on foot.' Miss Pink waited. 'I didn't cross the river at the bridge in the village but upstream a bit, so no one saw me. And I left Riffli and came back by the front door. Iris was in the kitchen with the telly, and Norman was working in the coach-house. Grandad had gone to bed long before.'

'Where was the Spitfire parked?'

Rachel gave a small nervous cough. 'I didn't notice. It was a dark night, no moon. Since Tony wasn't there, he'd probably taken the Spitfire.'

'You think he left before you arrived.'

'Hell! He wasn't in the cottage!'

'So the Spitfire wasn't there.'

'I can't say—' and now she was starting to lose control. Her voice rose: 'I wasn't looking for the bloody car; I was looking for her!'

'Why did you take the typescript? It wasn't in the filing cabinet and Thorne had no use for it.'

'The typescript,' Rachel said, with a return to composure, 'was actually on the bed. In fact, she was reading it.' A pause, then flatly: 'It provided the kindling.'

Miss Pink felt cold. She reached for the end of the sleeping bag and folded it over her wet thighs. 'So she denied having an affair with Norman,' she said conversationally. 'Why didn't you believe her?'

She could tell which questions were difficult to answer; the tension might not be tangible but it was obvious. Vibrations, she thought, and waited for an answer.

'The fog's coming in,' Rachel said. 'The light's going.'

The sea, which had been brilliant, was now dull and grey. There was no colour beyond the cavern mouth although the sun still shone. Samuel was sitting up straight and staring in their direction.

'Jakey slashed Norman's tyres,' Miss Pink

said thoughtfully.

After a while Rachel said. 'I can deal with Jakey. He's just a mixed-up kid.'

'Did you see him last night?'

'No!' There was movement and the girl was silhouetted against the light, peering out to sea. 'You'd better go.'

'Who are you hiding from?'

'The police. Who else?'

'You have to come out some time.'

'I shall.'

'When?'

'When I'm ready.'

'What good are you doing here, Rachel? Are you here for some purpose?'

The girl had drawn back in the corner. She didn't answer.

'What happened last night?' Miss Pink asked.

'Nothing.' It was quick but sullen.

'What! Iris naked on the kitchen table—covered with burns—and the poker in the fire!'

She heard the hiss of an indrawn breath, a gasp. The girl moved again.

'What do you want, Miss Pink?'

'Jakey has disappeared.'

'What's that go to do with me?'

'His clothes have been found on the beach.'

'What beach?'

'Why, in the bay: below Captain's Cottage.'

'Why was he killed?'

'If Jakey was the accomplice, the presumption would be that the person who murdered Sandra killed Jakey because he knew too much, wouldn't you say?'

'That sounds logical.'

'And yet, out of character,' Miss Pink observed. 'Sandra's death was quick, since she was unconscious when the cottage was set on fire, but drowning takes a long time.'

'Don't worry about that,' Rachel said with compassion, 'he was dead before he was put in the water.'

CHAPTER FOURTEEN

THE BIRDS WERE quiet as Miss Pink left the cavern, paddling close to the rock in order to avoid the wire. The boat was a blurred shadow on the perimeter of her vision with Samuel immobile in the stern. She was about to call to him when she heard a bizarre sound: the heavy thud of metal on metal, and it seemed to come from the sky. Echoes cracked across the cove like gunfire. For a moment she distrusted her hearing, then she struck out for the boat and saw Samuel turn towards her, his face a caricature of caution, a finger laid across his lips. She rested with her hands on the stern.

'There are men on top,' he whispered, 'bang on the edge of the cliff. I saw them before the fog closed in. They're climbers: helmets and ropes, but I think Pryce is with them. Listen!' Indecently loud in that claustrophobic world came the rhythmic blows of a hammer on iron. 'Where is she?' he hissed, peering past Miss Pink.

'She won't come out; I tried to persuade her but it was no good.'

'Why not?'

'She wouldn't give a reason.'

'I'll go in and tell her about the gang on top; she'll be caught like a rat—'

'But they're not after Rachel! If Pryce were trying to flush her out and using climbers to do it, they'd come down the slab. That's not easy, but every other line is impossible. But then if he wanted to reach the cavern, he'd do the same as us and come by boat.'

'What's he doing on top then?'

They had stopped whispering. Above them the noise continued and the gulls complained raucously. A little breeze got up, rocking the boat.

'He's sending someone down that shaft,' she said grimly. 'I want to see what's happening. Take me in for my clothes.'

'They'll hear when I start the engine.'

'You saw them so they have seen you. You're after lobsters. Start the engine; I'm cold.'

'And leave Rachel?'

'We have no choice.'

He took her to the shelf where she peeled off her swimsuit and dressed, blessing the forethought that had made her bring a heavy sweater. After the days of heat the fog was horribly chill.

She stepped back in the boat and Samuel

opened the throttle. They curved away to clear the reef. When they looked back they could see nothing, not even the portal of the great cave.

They pottered along the foot of the rock walls on a zig-zag course: going out for the reefs, coming in on the far side of them. They had no compass and they dared not lose sight of land, however forbiddingly it loomed above them. The only relief in that towering shade was the white plumage of the razor-bills.

They landed at Pentref's cove.

'But we can't leave the boat here,' Samuel protested. 'It'll be dark in half an hour with this fog.'

'Then it will have to stay overnight.'

They hid the outboard motor behind a rock and started up the ravine. Miss Pink walked fast and Samuel was too breathless to ask questions until they came out on the level ground where she had walked, yesterday with Rachel.

'What did she tell you?' he gasped.

'She confessed to the murder.'

'Never! Who's she protecting? Jakey, of course.'

'I hope so.'

'Why do you hope so?'

'It could mean he's still alive.'

His astonished eyes searched her face. 'Apart from that, did she tell you anything useful: anything that helps?'

'Oh yes.' She lengthened her stride.

'You do walk fast. What's the hurry?'

'I can't say—but things are speeding up; don't you feel it? As if someone's getting desperate, panicking. What has Pryce found in that shaft?'

'Oh, that's where the shaft is! You said it was a dead sheep.'

'Pritchard said there were no sheep here.'

A figure wavered in the gloom and her eyes narrowed as she recognised Carter, a pair of field glasses slung round his neck. None of them spoke. On the right a low bank showed against the background of space and she turned aside, Samuel trotting after her until he realised where he was and sat down abruptly like a stubborn dog. She continued alone down the miners' track.

The light was almost gone. At the foot of the track forms clustered like gargoyles on the edge of the abyss. At the sound of her footsteps they turned and she was aware of uniforms, and uniform expressions: pallor and the sweat of fear. They huddled inside the parapet as if it were a barricade against the depths. The farthest man was Pryce, and

234

Williams crouched behind him. A few feet away on the ledge at the top of the shaft stood two men in climbing gear. They wore leather gauntlets and they were taking the strain of taut ropes running into the shaft.

'Evening,' Pryce announced in an artificial voice. 'Just your scene, this.'

'You do get around,' Miss Pink said. 'Who is it?' but she knew.

A bony hand appeared on the lip of the shaft and light gleamed on red helmet.

'It's twisting,' a voice said. 'Wait—heave when he comes clear—when I say.'

'Don't damage him!' Pryce cried.

'Hell, man, you can't help it,' exclaimed one of the men at the top. The other asked coldly: 'How would you like to come and do the job yourself?' No one answered him. In the silence Miss Pink thought she could hear the tide-race running.

The third rescuer moved up, supported by his toes and a taut rope, straining at something which had not yet showed and which no one, basically, wanted to see.

There was a pale flash, pale brown, humped, with the backbone prominent, and then the rest of it, naked. They hoisted it over the edge, still in that rigid hooped position but one arm, the left, twisted back, revealing the ribs streaked and caked with dry blood. It was Jakey and he had been stabbed.

There was a change in the atmosphere and as Miss Pink tried to identify it she was aware of the colour: of blue—and the vividness of shirts and helmets, of green ferns in cracks. She saw that Pryce's eyes were frantic with the compulsion to step forward and terror of the drop—and this jumble of impressions was pierced by a thread of sound: urgent, commanding. On the skyline a man was shouting and pointing, pointing down.

The fog hadn't gone; it had merely parted. Below them was a glimpse of wrinkled water, of birds like drifting snowflakes, and of the slab with more fog rolling up the rock and a figure in jeans and a white shirt creeping in front of it.

The figure stepped out on top, glanced casually towards the funnel and was swallowed up in the cloud.

Pryce looked at his men and they looked back at him stonily. There was nothing he could do. Only climbers could follow her and he had no justification for asking them to do so.

Miss Pink started up the track but before she'd gone a few yards he caught her up, slithering in town shoes. He passed, very red in the face, and she plodded behind, almost dawdling but her mind racing.

Samuel stood at the top of the track, his eyes on Pryce's retreating back. He turned to Miss Pink.

'What was Carter shouting about?'

'Rachel climbed out and made off towards Pentref.' His eyes widened in delight but she was grim. 'And Jakey was in the shaft. Stabbed.'

'Christ!'

The fog was thick again. She led the way to the stile.

'Do we do anything about Rachel?' he asked.

'She can take care of herself on this ground. Let's find Pryce.'

They found him in the first field beyond the boundary bank, where there was a group of cars. He was using the radio on one of them while Carter stood at the open door, listening attentively.

Pryce finished and stood up. He was as pale now as he'd been flushed before. 'I'm sealing this place off,' he said. 'I've sent for more cars.'

'Why?' Samuel exploded.

Pryce showed no surprise at his vehemence. 'There's been two murders, and the killer—'

237

he looked from Samuel to Carter reflectively, '—is still here. So are several witnesses who haven't talked yet—like that boy.' He gestured towards the funnel. 'And,' he added softly, 'like Mrs Kemp, whom I've not had the opportunity of talking to as yet.'

'You've eliminated Thorne?' Miss Pink asked curiously.

'How many killers have we got?' They accepted this as rhetorical. He continued, with an air of conscious drama: 'Thorne was picked up in Dover last night, trying to get across the Channel on a false passport. He was identified this afternoon.' He turned to Carter. 'And who are you, sir?'

'My name is Carter. I was Sandra Maitland's agent.'

Pryce's face didn't change but he was holding his breath. 'Indeed,' he said at last, 'and you have something to tell me, Mr Carter.' It wasn't a question. He looked hard at Miss Pink who returned the look blandly, nodded and turned away. Samuel fell into step beside her.

They went to Riffli where they found Roderick with Norman in the drawing room. Miss Pink was shocked to see how tired everyone looked—except for Iris, pouring brandy competently and without orders, handing

238

Miss Pink, a generous measure with a predictable: 'That'll do you good; you look as if you've had a long day.'

'Have yer seen Rachel?' Roderick barked.

'We have.'

'Good. Where is she?'

'On the cliffs.'

'Huh. Did she come home with yer?'

'No.'

'Couldn't you get her to come home?' Norman asked, his tone resigned.

'No.'

'Yer a bit curt, Melinda; what's on yer mind, eh?'

'Rachel. She confessed to the murder.'

Norman gasped. 'What—'

'Rubbish!' Iris turned back from the door as she was about to leave. 'She's having you on.'

'Fantasising,' Norman said.

Roderick was blinking at them. He turned to Miss Pink. 'Why'd she say that, Mel?' His tone was mildly curious.

She shrugged and smiled. Samuel's face was blank.

'If you ask my opinion,' Iris said heavily, 'she's protecting that young imp, Jakey Jones. He's in London right now, you mark my words. Those clothes on the beach wouldn't

239

fool a baby.'

'So you reckon he joined up with Thorne, do you?' Norman asked. 'Always one for the main chance: that's our Jakey. And if Thorne's selling Sandra's book, Jakey'll be there for his cut.'

'I doubt it,' Miss Pink said.

'Oh, *you* don't think he went to London?' he asked with interest.

Roderick leaned back against the sofa, watching her.

'He's dead,' she said. 'He was stabbed last night and the body put down the old mine shaft on the headland.'

Norman gaped at her. They were all silent until Roderick barked: 'What's that mean?'

'Thorne.' Norman swallowed. 'He came back.'

'He was in custody last night,' Miss Pink said. 'The police caught him at Dover.'

Iris said unhappily: 'This will be the death of Thirza. Someone ought to be with her.'

'Caradoc's there.' Norman gnawed a thumb nail. 'I'm thinking of Rachel. Does she know about Jakey?'

'She saw us all gathered round the shaft,' Miss Pink said. 'With the rescuers there she'd draw her own conclusions.'

'She'll be all right,' Roderick said comfortably. 'How was Jakey killed?'

'He was stabbed.'

'Ah yes, so yer said. Any weapon in the shaft?'

'I didn't wait.'

'Who'd kill Jakey?' Norman asked.

Samuel spoke for the first time. 'Anyone. You, me—anyone who'd suffered from his sadism, but actually I expect it was the chap who killed Sandra.' He grinned and his eyes were wild. 'I'm going home. We don't have to bother about it any more; Pryce may not get his man, but Carter will. You haven't seen his eyes.' He walked out of the room.'

Iris said: 'Mr Honey is so sensitive. . . .'

★   ★   ★

Miss Pink lay steaming in a hot bath, considering ideas and loose ends. At Pentref's cove there was a boat; at Parry's Lobster's cottage: her car. If Rachel came across the car she might not recognise it but the boat was a different matter, and she'd have the intelligence to find the outboard motor. What was to be made of it if she escaped? And if she stayed voluntarily? And how was one to know that she'd made a choice, or that she merely hadn't come across the boat?

She considered the possible significance of Jakey's clothes—his jeans and shoes—being found in almost the same place as the kitten. A man like Samuel could and would kill if he came on Jakey torturing a cat, particularly Caithness, but there were two factors against Samuel's having killed Jakey. One was that he hadn't been carrying a knife last night, not a large one anyway, and the fatal wound had been made by something long and quite wide. The second point in his favour was that he could hardly have carried the body from the beach to the headland—nor would he have the nerve to go down the funnel. . . .

A voice asked quietly: 'Are you there, Miss Pink?'

She stared at the window. 'Who is it?'

'Pryce. Can I have a word?'

She dressed reluctantly and opened the front door. He was alone.

'It's midnight,' she said pointedly as they sat down. 'Are you going to work all night?'

'I'll get a few hours sleep on a camp bed at the hotel. I've sent for the trailer we use as a control centre but that won't get here till first light, and we can't do anything on the cliffs until daylight.' He settled himself in his chair and beamed, drooping but once again affable. She thought that perhaps he hadn't been so much hostile on the cliffs as frightened of the ground. 'What was Honey's motive?' he asked.

She was surprised but only mildly so. 'I was pondering that in my bath—but Jakey wasn't killed on the beach, Samuel wasn't carrying the weapon last night, and he's terrified of heights.' She beamed back at him.

'Indeed.' His grin was ferocious. 'But I was thinking of a motive for killing Sandra.'

'Oh, Sandra.' She shrugged. This was a point where a hostess might offer refreshment but she felt it was important not to do so at this moment. Instead she asked: 'Why Samuel?'

'You know that.'

'Of course; you saw him in the cove, and someone told you that we arrived at the mines together. Yes, I was with him in the cove but our being there had no connection with your being on top. There's a cavern underneath that shaft and Rachel Kemp was in it.'

'Why?'

'I don't know.'

'I never thought to hear you answer a question in that way, ma'am.'

'I don't know all the answers. I mean to discover that one though: why she was hiding in the cavern.'

'So she was hiding.'

'Yes. And she's on the run from you now.' She was equable. 'She's frightened, but not of you.'

'I take it you don't know who she's frightened of. Could it be Jakey?'

She saw the trap and side-stepped it in the only way possible. 'I couldn't get her to talk.'

'I never met young Jakey,' he said wistfully, 'but I know all about him. Some talked: like Myfanwy Hughes; but she talked to make sure no suspicion touched her boy. Of course, she alibis Ossie for the night of the fire but a mother's alibi can be as valueless as a wife's. That's immaterial here; Ossie knew nothing about the fire. He couldn't keep any secret, let alone one that involved murder. I was saying: Myfanwy talked about Jakey—and so did the local police officer, but no one else did. Significant, eh?'

'He was the worst type of delinquent.'

'And you should know.'

'How did you know where to look for the body?' she asked curiously.

'We had a phone call, not really anonymous; it was from Carter but he didn't get

244

around to giving his name at the time. Perhaps he was waiting to see what was in the hole. He told me he was the caller when he introduced himself after we got the body up. He's talked.'

'And how did he know there was anything in the shaft?'

'He watched you earlier in the day.'

'But Samuel Honey waited for me at the top.'

'Carter had glasses. And there's cover; the gorse is quite high. My guess is that he watched your movements and, when you'd gone, duplicated them. He was right about the shaft.'

'*My* reaction was that a sheep had fallen in.'

'Different minds. The urban mentality immediately thought of a human body, particularly when clothes had been found abandoned. Now we know why there was no shirt with Jakey's jeans; if he was killed with his clothes on, there'd be a cut in the material.'

'And blood.'

'Yes. Somewhere there's a lot of blood. Where would you look for it, ma'am?'

She took care with her answer while he watched her intently.

'If it were premeditated,' she said, 'you might expect him to have been killed in the sea, but—' she recalled her musing in the bath, '—it's too far to carry the body: from the bay to the headland. So he could—might have been killed in a bath. . . . Most unlikely: you can't inveigle a clothed boy into a bath—and he was clothed because the shirt's missing?' She raised her eyebrows at her own question. 'A compromise would be to kill him out of doors but on land, not in water; earth would soak up the blood. It's still there of course, but less obvious.'

'Than what, ma'am?' The tone was intimate.

'Less obvious than indoors.'

They regarded each other in silence. They were both exhausted; Miss Pink had reached the stage where she was running on second wind and she felt clear-headed and hardly tired at all except that when she considered making coffee, her leg muscles signalled a protest before they received an impulse from the brain.

'You know Carter's story,' he said pleasantly. She nodded. 'You didn't tell me.'

'What proof was there that it was true?'

'But whatever credence you put—or didn't put on it, here was the agent. You held that

246

back.'

'Was it important?'

He ignored that. 'And Honey: he knew.' She was silent. 'You've got something to hide too?' he asked. 'I'm bringing Thorne back; if that story's true, with him here we may find proof of it. Traces, for instance, and tracks. Thorne's got a record, by the way: house-breaking.' He shot her a glance. 'No doubt you've found where the Spitfire was parked.'

'Where *a* car was parked,' she amended. 'Carter postulates two killers: signalling with torches; that's possible too.'

'Thank you, ma'am.' He was heavily ironical. 'So if Thorne's out of it—and we know he didn't kill Jakey Jones—we've got two killers here, or one left alive—' He paused but she waited attentively, without comment. 'The fire was set in the bedroom,' he went on quietly, and she stiffened. They were back with Sandra. She wondered if he were being deliberately confusing: switching from one murder to the other without preamble. 'And I'm wondering,' he was saying, 'if Thorne will tell us that one key of the filing cabinet was in Sandra's handbag. He'd have a second key himself. Carter says there were two keys. So the girl would be hit over the head, the key taken, then the book, and the killer would go back upstairs to set the fire. The book may have been burned then.'

Miss Pink's eyes flickered. 'What makes you think that?'

'Because I reckon that book's a red herring. It's got relevance but not in the obvious way. No prominent politician came speeding down here to kill her to avoid exposure, because the story hadn't broken; it wasn't in the papers until the following day and then she was dead. But the book was the handle that got the Press down here. At first I thought the Press were being used to complicate matters, even to widen the circle of suspects. I've changed my mind. When that call was put through to Fleet Street on the night of Bowen's birthday party, the caller intended to drive Sandra Maitland away, not to kill her.'

'How can you know all this?'

'I don't. It's a theory. What do you think of it?'

'It's reasonable.'

'It narrows the circle. The killer has to be someone who knew about the book. According to Caradoc Jones, that was everyone at the birthday party.' He paused. 'Which contradicts Carter's story; you told him you didn't know about the book.'

'I was giving nothing away to Carter,' she

said stoutly. 'For all I knew, he could be the killer himself—'

'No; he was on a plane when Sandra was killed.'

She compressed her lips, then said: 'Sandra did tell us that she was writing a book; not all of us, Rachel had gone to bed.'

'She *wasn't* told?'

'Her husband told her in the morning.'

'*He* says.' It was a statement, not a question. His tone changed. 'The Fleet Street call was intended as a frightener: to make her go. Sandra was a danger to someone in Abersaint; someone at that party. Carter hasn't the slightest doubt who that is. Two killers, ma'am, and the only person Jakey Jones would have consented to work with is Rachel Kemp. Even Caradoc—whose mind isn't working properly right now—says that 'everyone's hand was turned against him, except Miss Rachel's'. His words. Have you anything to say to that?'

'She didn't kill Jakey; she could have done it, she's got the temperament, but she didn't.'

'How do you know?'

'Character,' she lied.

He was angry. 'What happened last night: when she came roaring down to the quay in a Mini?'

'Well, she certainly didn't kill Jakey at Riffli; her husband and the housekeeper were about and the place was blazing with light.'

'So what frightened her?'

'She saw a huge Alsatian in the woods—' She stopped her face expressionless.

He stood up. 'And came down to the village instead of going to the house for her husband? She can't get away; the peninsula's sealed off and we'll search those cliffs tomorrow.'

'Who will search the cliffs?' She put the faintest emphasis on the pronoun.

'We'll get professional rescuers in, like we did for the body.'

'On what grounds can you call them in? That's she's a suspect?'

'You know better than that. No; I'm worried that I've lost a witness in a murder case. She may be lying injured down a hole, even in the sea. I'll have boats out tomorrow too, fog or no fog.' He smiled without amusement. 'And now I'll leave you, ma'am; I hope you sleep well.'

CHAPTER FIFTEEN

PRYCE'S VEILED THREAT had no effect on Miss Pink who slept badly only when there were decisions to be worked out, and before he'd come to Captain's Cottage she'd decided on her first move the following morning. She woke with a fine awareness of restored energy but, glancing at the window in the wish for a clear bright day to confirm her mood, she received a shock; there was no brilliance behind the curtains.

It was six o'clock. The visible world was demarcated by the fuchsia hedge, every leaf and bloom hung with drops of moisture. She thought of the headland smothered in this . . . but it was high summer and the fog would surely disintegrate later. That could make things easier for Pryce.

A change came sooner than she anticipated. There was a strong breeze blowing when she crossed the green after an early breakfast. Along the mountain ridge lay a thick band of cloud, its depths shadowless and still, its edges shredded by air currents. Great wraiths of cloud sped down the gullies, whirling and spinning towards the village where the sun was blazing, and a breath of icy air travelled before the cloud like wind before an avalanche.

No one was abroad except Miss Pink. There was a line of cars parked on the quay but no marked police vehicles. Soon the roads would be jammed but for the moment it appeared that she was the only person awake in Abersaint.

She strode purposefully up the valley and into the shadow of the trees. Birds sang, the river ran noisily on her left, and on the slopes above, the cloud gyrated madly down the screes.

On the left of the lane was a bank covered with harebells. There was no verge, nowhere for a car to park until one came to the turning for the mill cottage and there a notice proclaimed that the woods were private land. Past the entrance there was a stone stile on the river side of the lane leading to one of those tiny overgrown paddocks. Something had passed through the bracken recently; there were one or two broken stalks but no animal tracks showed in the lush grass.

Miss Pink stood at the top of the bank and looked down through tree trunks to stepping stones in shallow water with muddy margins—and to Avril Pritchard trampling the mud in her heavy brogues, peering at the ground as if she had dropped a small but valuable object.

'Lost something?' Miss Pink said as she slithered down the bank.

Avril showed no surprise to see her at such an early hour. She smiled without subterfuge.

'Have you seen a red and white bullock?'

'No. Have you lost one?' Miss Pink held the girl's eye. 'What kind of tracks would it leave?' They studied the ground intently. 'Someone was here before you.' Miss Pink pointed to the imprint of a ridged sole. The soles of Avril's shoes were cleated and the marks of those were everywhere.

'Are you looking for Rachel?' the girl asked.

'Not yet. The police will be after her today. Tell her to take care on those cliffs.'

Avril nodded. 'I'll do that—if I see her. 'Bye now.'

''Bye,' Miss Pink returned absently, looking where Avril had been standing, shifting her feet. The mark of the ridged sole was quite obliterated.

*   *   *

'She was here in the small hours,' Samuel

said, pouring her a cup of coffee in his kitchen. 'She's running rings round the police.'

'It's not the police I'm bothered about,' Miss Pink said, 'at least, not directly, but if they've sealed the peninsula effectively and they've trapped the killer, then he's trapped with her.'

'"He"?'

'Or she. Why did Rachel come to you? To find out something, I'll be bound. If she'd only talk, I wouldn't be so worried about her. How did she get to you without the police seeing, anyway? There was someone in the graveyard before I turned in.'

'There was a patrol car on the green too. Rachel waited until the chaps in the graveyard went down on the beach, then she came through your garden and the tombstones and climbed the downpipe to my bedroom window.' He giggled. She realised with amazement that he was enjoying this. 'Caithness woke me,' he said: 'growling. A guardkitten, so help me.'

'What did she say?'

'She wanted to know what the police were doing at the shaft. Dead give-away, wasn't it? Of course, Pryce would say it was a superb bit of double-bluff but if she'd killed Jakey, she'd tell me and be absolutely certain that I'd die with her secret intact—' Suddenly he was serious. 'So who did kill him? But we know, don't we?'

'Not necessarily; it could be any member of her family—or you.'

He was unperturbed. 'So I know it's one of the others.' Then he added flatly: 'But I don't believe it. You've gone wrong somewhere.'

'I'd like to think so,' she said. 'Did you tell her to take the boat from Pentref's cove?'

'She'd found it already but Pryce got there first. He must have guessed we'd beached it as close as possible and he'd have some local men with him. The rescuers were local. He'd put a guard on the boat.'

'If she meant to go, she could have slipped across the road in the fog. Even if there were half a dozen patrol cars up there, dodging them would have been child's play for her.'

'She didn't *want* to go. I tried to persuade her: for laughs, I said: dodging the fuzz; she wasn't interested. She's got something in mind.'

'That worries me too,' Miss Pink said helplessly. 'What was her reaction when you told her it was Jakey's body in the shaft?'

'She didn't turn a hair—'

'Coming clean,' Miss Pink murmured. 'She sent Avril Pritchard to erase the tracks the killer left on the river bank. The killer didn't use a car—I'm talking about Sandra now, not Jakey—and there were tracks. Rachel said she made them going back to Riffli so I went to look. I saw one print: of a ridged tennis shoe or track shoe but the owner had slipped. It didn't appear large; it could have been a boy's track, or a woman's, or a man's with small feet. Avril managed to obliterate that one as well.'

'Crossing the river would mean going back to Riffli,' he said grimly.

'Or the hotel—in order to dodge the bridge in the village. Norman—' she said, mentioning the name that had been hovering on the rim of their consciousness, '—has an alibi for the time of Sandra's murder. We are working on the premise that both murders were done by the same person so that if a person has an alibi for one death, they appear to be in the clear. Norman has an alibi for Sandra; I'd hazard a guess that Doreen and Rupert have alibis for Jakey. Of course, that does depend when Jakey was killed—' She pondered; was she missing something here?

'Roderick was immobilised on the night of Sandra's murder,' Samuel contributed, 'and so we're back to Square One and everybody's guilty again.'

Miss Pink looked at him as if she were surfacing from an anaesthetic. A tearing sound of claws on cretonne came from the living room. They ignored it.

'Why is she on tranquillisers?' she asked.

He shook his head helplessly. 'I—don't—know. I've never known. She used to tell me everything, and now she's withdrawn; she's on the defensive. Even last night she was tight as a spring but still in control, even if the control was paper-thin. She wasn't giving anything away.'

'She used to come to you before she was married: during the nuclear campaign?'

'Lord, yes! We were living in each other's pockets then. Terrific fun; sometimes we were up most of the night planning.'

'You never got depressed?'

'Not with Roderick around. How could we?' He stopped and thought about this. 'Subconsciously it must have had its effect on Rachel though because Norman says she dreams about it: Hiroshima, you know, and the radiation burns . . . Burns,' he repeated thoughtfully, and stared at her. 'Norman says she sleeps badly, and then there's this thing she's got about the Longheads; it used not to be like that: the cannibalism bit. . . . There's a very unhealthy atmosphere around here,

257

don't you think? Horrible deaths, this recurrent motif of fire and burns; it's not surprising that she's on tranquillisers. All the same,' he added, 'she was remarkably sane last night; balanced, I mean. You'd never have thought there was anything wrong, except—'

'Except what?'

'She seemed—ruthless. That's new. Now, if she'd been like this before, someone who didn't know her might be justified in considering her as a murder suspect, but up till now she's been passionate, lost—floundering, I thought, in something—God knows what. Bewildered, she seemed. Last night she wasn't. She frightened me.'

He drove her to Cae Coch for her car. The fog had gone. There was a patrol car in the lay-by at the road junction, another near the turning to Cae Coch. Expressionless drivers watched them pass and on the rising ground north of the main road were stationary figures sited in such a fashion that, with binoculars, they must have the length of the road in view from bay to bay.

'She could be on the mountain,' Samuel said.

'There's no cover on the mountain,' she responded absently. 'She could hide under a rock but she'd have to move in front of a sweep search and then she'd be visible immediately to watchers below the mountain. It would be like beating a wood; the quarry's got to show. So she'll stay on the cliffs—' she glanced sideways at him, '—unless she's made other arrangements.'

'Not to my knowledge.'

She left him at Cae Coch, placating Parry Lobsters who, with the peasant's unfailing instinct for drama, maintained that his boat was lost although he'd known, since Samuel informed him last night, that it was beached in Pentref's cove. She drove back to the village and Riffli. Norman Kemp appeared at the back door as her car entered the yard. She greeted him affably and asked for Roderick. He was telephoning in the passage. She nodded and walked past and out to the front lawn. Norman did not follow.

After a few moments Roderick joined her and they stood with their backs to the house looking down through the Scots pines to the sparkling sea.

'That was Pryce on the phone,' he said. 'He's sending for a rescue team to search the cliffs now that the fog's gone. The climbers will do the slopes; his own men will be on the top.'

'What's he searching for?'

259

'The weapon, he said. They're going along the bottom too, in boats. She'll dodge 'em.' He twinkled at her. 'Oh yes, I know what's in his mind; he thinks she's a killer.' He gave a cackle of laughter.

'When did you change your mind?' she asked pleasantly.

His amusement died and he glowered at her. 'Always knew she had nothing to do with it.'

'With what?'

'Why, that poor girl. As for Jakey Jones—' he shrugged, '—could have been anyone.'

'What about the branch on the granary steps?'

'Yes.' He was sombre. 'That was probably Jakey.'

'Why did you retract? At first you said it was an attempt on your life but after Sandra died you said you'd been mistaken.'

'Didn't want ter attract attention,' he mumbled. 'Sensed trouble when we found that cottage burned out, and she'd never tried ter get off the bed even. None of that had anything ter do with an attempt on me own life, of course, but the police would be interested if they knew about the branch and me fall, however much of a coincidence it was. Didn't want attention focused on Riffli at that

260

moment.'

'Because of Rachel.' It was a statement of fact.

He was embarrassed. 'Bad enough for Pryce ter know Sandra came ter me party; no need for him ter know anything else.'

'What made Rachel so hostile to her?'

He snorted and muttered under his breath. She caught something about 'wild oats'. She said firmly. 'Rachel has never given any indication to me of being unbalanced.'

'Of course not!' he exploded. 'Just a touch of nerves.' He looked uncomfortable. 'That's Iris's term for it, but Rachel don't talk much to us, yer know; Norman comes in for most of it. He's a good feller; he can handle it although it seems ter be getting him down of late. Nothing in the story about Sandra, yer know; Rachel's a bit possessive, that's all.'

'As with Jakey.'

A ladybird alighted on his wrist and he studied it with intense interest.

'Feudal?' she hazarded. He looked lost. 'The Bowens haven't forgotten a time when they were the law,' she told him.

His face was all innocence. 'Yer not taken in by that! Delusions of grandeur aren't in our line. She didn't take the law into her own hands and kill Jakey.'

'She'd have some difficulty carrying him to the funnel certainly.'

'Not if he was killed on the cliffs,' he said absently, then raised his head and looked at her without expression.

'She'd take the knife with her?' She smiled. So did he. 'Does blood worry her?' she asked, as if on a new tack.

He blinked. 'No; now that you ask: no. Why?'

'What about injured animals? Does she panic?'

'Of course not; she helps Pritchard, or did before her marriage. She's very handy on the farm: lambing, calving, not in the least squeamish. You can't be on a farm; some of the sights are very unpleasant: blow-fly maggots, fractures. Common sense, most of it; First Aid's a help—yer can adapt, improvise.'

'Rachel's done First Aid?' she asked idly.

'Not Rachel, no. I'm the First Aider,' he said proudly, puffing out his chest. 'I'm the local secretary; we get a St John's chap to run lectures in the winter.'

'Here?'

'Right here, at Riffli. We've no village hall, d'yer see. That's why Pryce has had to bring in his mobile murder centre, or whatever he calls it. Great caravan, down on the quay.

How much d'yer bet someone won't take the brake off and it falls in the water?'

'You're very cheerful.'

He walked away a few steps, then turned back to her. 'How d'yer expect me to behave? Run round like a hen with its head chopped off bleating: "Who did it"? I don't know who did it but I'm going out on those cliffs and see what's happening. They're not hunting me own kin over me own land without me being there ter see fair play. I'm taking me shot gun—'

'*What!*'

'—ter pot a rabbit.'

★   ★   ★

'I'll cut some sandwiches,' Iris said, 'but if you're going out on those cliffs, I'm going with you. There've been enough accidents.'

Norman gaped at her. Miss Pink said: 'We'll all go; I'll run down and pick up Rupert too.'

'I'll ring Samuel,' Roderick said, and walked out of the kitchen. Norman stared at Miss Pink with anguished eyes.

'Why don't you go and have a lie-down for a while,' Iris urged. 'You've been up most of the night—'

He ignored her and appealed to Miss Pink.

'I'm terrified of her state of mind. . . . It's got to stop: the drugs and the booze; she doesn't know where she is half the time—'

'It'll work out.' Iris slapped slices of bread on the table, buttering them with careless efficiency. 'She's got everything going for her: family, friends, a lovely home. . . .'

He sighed heavily. 'I can't reach her; she goes wandering all over those cliffs in the middle of the night—'

'Not all that often,' Iris put in quickly. A look flashed between them. 'Moonlit nights,' she stressed. 'She's romantic. She doesn't go out when there's no moon. She was in Wednesday and Thursday, you see.'

'Those were the nights of the murders,' Miss Pink said.

Norman shrugged. 'Well, it gives her an alibi—for what it's worth.'

'Don't joke about it,' Iris said reprovingly. 'She never set foot outside this house on Thursday night.'

'Except when she came down to the quay in the Mini,' Miss Pink pointed out.

'I mean before then. I had a lot to do that evening so I was all over the place. I saw her several times.'

'I had a drink with her at one point,'

Norman said. 'And then we all watched a programme for a while: in the dining room because it was so hot in here. Then she went
upstairs and she didn't come down again because she'd have had to pass the dining room
door and that was wide open to catch a
draught.'

'Where were you when she ran out of the
house?' Miss Pink asked. He looked blank.

'With the telly on you wouldn't hear her
come down,' Iris said. 'You wouldn't hear the
engine if there was a noisy scene. I heard the
engine. That's odd. . . . Oh, I remember; I
was in the downstairs toilet. It's got a window
on the yard.'

'Yer never told us what she dreamed
about,' Roderick barked from the doorway. 'I
was going to ask her in the morning but she'd
gone. What was it, Mel?'

Miss Pink said: 'It was the kind of hallucination you'd get with something like LSD; it
doesn't seem to equate with a tranquilliser.'

'LSD?' Norman gasped, and turned to Iris.

She shook her head. She was packaging
sandwiches neatly in greaseproof paper. 'I
know all about Thursday night,' she said.
'Rachel told me in the morning. It was a kind
of nightmare—nasty, yes, but they don't
have to worry their heads about it, do they,

Miss Pink?'

Roderick and Norman started to shout at her, then stopped. Iris placidly worked elastic bands round her packages. 'Least said, soonest mended,' she observed.

'Iris!' Norman's tone was dangerous. 'There's a murderer loose in this village.'

'Well, I don't know—' she cast a doubtful glance at the window, '—it's not very nice; I'm glad that fog's gone.'

It silenced them, until Roderick said flatly: 'It's not; there's another bank to the south. Shouldn't be surprised if it comes in much earlier today. What d'yer say, Mel; shall we go out to the Head?'

She hesitated.

'I'm coming, Rod,' Norman said firmly.

'Right, lad; I'll get me gun.'

'Your what?'

They turned towards the window as they heard the sound of an engine coming up the drive. A car came into the yard and Samuel got out.

'I'd better make some more sandwiches,' Iris said, as if it were a tea party.

'You'll come too?' Miss Pink pressed. 'She'll listen to you.'

Fear leapt in Norman's eyes. 'Of course she'll come! She's got to come! She's like a

mo—well, like one of the family to Rachel.'
He was trembling.

'Look,' Iris said firmly, 'nothing's going to happen; she's just doing it for laughs, that's all: making monkeys of the police—' Norman made a stricken gesture. 'All right,' she said soothingly, 'of course I'm coming; maybe it won't be a bad thing to have all the family—' Her eyes moved to the doorway. Samuel was standing there, obviously bewildered by the conversation.

'Everyone's going up on the cliffs?' he asked, as if trying to understand a new development.

'Everyone.' Miss Pink walked over to him, conveying a message which only he could see. He followed her out to the yard where she opened the driver's door of her car, stooped to the seat catch, then stepped aside.

'See if you can push it forward,' she ordered, and walked round to the passenger door. They struggled with the seat lever, their heads below the dashboard.

'Keep close to Roderick,' she whispered. 'Don't let anyone else come near him, nor between you. If you can get hold of his gun, do that; you'll look like an armed bodyguard. And keep back from the edge. Don't stare at me; struggle with that lever.'

The seat plunged forward. 'Who d'you think—'

'I'm not sure.'

'Why don't you come? Two of us would be much better.'

'I have to go to the hotel.'

'Hell! Is that more important than Roderick's life? And what about Rachel? Or—Oh, no!'

'There's something else I have to do. I want you to make sure they all leave Riffli. Hang around until the last one's gone—but keep Roderick with you if you have to do that. Now go in and get them moving.'

★   ★   ★

Abersaint was now the centre of a double murder investigation and the hotel bar was so crowded that people were drinking outside, on the quay. There was an air of carnival, macabre against the background of flamboyant police cars, the yellow vans of telephone engineers and the big white trailer opposite the fish sheds. Beyond Riffli's hanging woods the fog was a milky smear obscuring the horizon. Miss Pink frowned as she got out of her car. It could go either way in the fog.

The big reporter called Waterhouse was

talking to Rupert in the bar.

'Where's Pryce?' she asked without pre-amble.

'He could be with Thorne or Carter.' Waterhouse was equally business-like.

'Has Carter been arrested?'

'Not that I know of. What would the charge be?' He looked pensive. 'I'm not a crime man; something to do with suppressing evidence vital to a murder inquiry, or not reporting a death? There's a road block at the top of the lane,' he added, lowering his head like an animal about to charge.

'There wasn't earlier this morning.'

'Been out then?' He grinned wolfishly.

'I had business to attend to.' She was on her dignity. 'Is there any news of the murder weapon?'

'The last murder?' He was pretending to be naive. 'It could have been a chef's knife.' His eyes slewed to Rupert who looked bored.

'A lot of people in Abersaint would have a chef's knife,' Rupert said. 'There's even one in Miss Pink's cottage.'

'So there is.' She was genuinely surprised.

'The killer must have been covered with blood,' Waterhouse observed generally. 'Who changed his clothes late that evening?'

'Unless he did it naked,' said a stranger at

his elbow: a tall thin man with sharp eyes.

'That's not so fool-proof as is made out,' Miss Pink said. 'It takes a long time to wash off blood, and what happens to footprints on the way to the bathroom?' She considered the other point. 'Everyone I saw appeared to be wearing the same clothes throughout the evening—' she smiled, '—but is it likely I saw the killer?'

'Is it likely you'd know?' asked the sharp man.

She stirred uneasily and glanced at Rupert. 'I would have come in here after dinner on Thursday—'

'You didn't.' His face was expressionless. 'I don't know what time you finished your dinner but you didn't come in the bar and I was here all night.' His eye wandered casually to the man who was a stranger to Miss Pink.

'That's correct,' he acknowledged. 'Mr Bowen was in here continually—which gives him an alibi, but not yourself, miss, ha ha!' It was facetious, in bad taste, and totally at variance with the careful eyes. She smiled politely.

'And Carter dined here?' she asked.

'Thursday and last night,' Rupert said slowly. 'He eats here but I don't know where he's staying.'

'He sleeps in his car,' Waterhouse announced. They stared at him.

'Leaves him free to roam, doesn't it?' put in the stranger. Miss Pink decided he was a plainclothes policeman.

She left the bar and went to the Bowens' quarters where she found Doreen dusting in the sitting room. She wasted no time.

'What made you think Norman was having an affair with Sandra Maitland?' she asked.

Doreen was astonished but she recovered quickly and her eyes narrowed.

'I jumped to conclusions.'

'Rachel was never specific about it?'

'No; she's far too loyal. But something was wrong; you saw her at the party.'

'How did you discover it wasn't Sandra?'

'Rachel told me; she said she loathed Sandra but in general terms, not because there was anything between her and Norman. She said Norman was terrified of Sandra.'

'When did she tell you that?'

Doreen smiled and her eyes were quite friendly towards Miss Pink. 'Well, you can guess when, can't you? Thursday, yesterday? It's immaterial. It was after suspicion started that Sandra had been murdered, of course.'

★   ★   ★

271

'We all knew what she was,' Caradoc said woodenly, stroking his satchel strap with fingers that needed something to do.

'You discussed her among yourselves,' Miss Pink prompted, 'her diamonds, her furs—and at the time you thought she'd gate-crashed the party?'

'She had a death wish. She was trying to destroy herself; no need to try, she was rotten at the core. A psychopath, she was: completely irresponsible. That book. . . . I mean, who'd talk about a book like that in decent company? The death wish. We said she was mad.'

'You realised it that night.'

'Not just me: all of us. I mean, Mrs Jones is one person and Mrs MacNally's another. We were all agreed on it.'

'And the ladies didn't even see her.'

'Course they did. Went round to the front and watched through the drawing room window, didn't they?' He swallowed and looked past Miss Pink's attentive face to the white trailer beyond the police cars. 'Mrs Jones had never set eyes on her; she had to see her that night to find out what she were like. It was important to Mrs Jones.'

'But she didn't make a scene.'

'Well, Mrs MacNally was with her,' Caradoc said.

CHAPTER SIXTEEN

BEFORE THE DRIVE ran into Riffli's yard, a
cart track which was little more than two ruts
struck off to the right. Miss Pink turned along
this and, leaving her car hidden in the undergrowth, she continued through the woods on
foot until there was only a screen of rhododendrons between herself and the cobbled
yard.

The place was silent except for swallows
twittering in the eaves. The kitchen windows
were wide and a curtain hung over the sill.
The back door was closed.

She took a deep breath and, stepping out of
the shrubbery, advanced to the window. The
kitchen was untenanted: a loaf on the table,
butter in its opened pack, cheese, pickles, used
cutlery. The untidiness was disturbing.

She entered the house without stealth and
went along the passage. She opened the dairy
door, switched on the light and crossed the
flags to the freezer. Lifting the lid she contem-
plated the space above the jumbled packages.
Incongruously, in the circumstances, the
thought occurred to her that the Bowens lived
well.

In the kitchen she surveyed the clutter, moving the greasy butter pack and some slices of bread to expose a crack in the wooden table. Like all cracks in old tables, and most unhygienically, it held a kind of dry black mud where the scrubbing brush didn't penetrate.

She inspected the floor—gleaming dully from constant washing, the cooker, the walls, the legs of the table. She even stepped back to peer at the ceiling above the clothes rack. The rack was hung with the product of a day's wash: linen, overalls, shirts, all neatly ironed and folded.

The room darkened. She glanced at the window and saw the sunlight go flitting through the trees, chased by shadow. Then she heard the sound of an engine. She went quickly along the passage and up the stairs to the landing where all the windows were open. Now she identified the engine as that of an aeroplane and sighed with relief.

She went through the rooms selectively, ignoring the one which was obviously Roderick's, but spending quite a while on the bookshelves in that shared by Norman and Rachel. Then she passed Roderick's room to the end of the corridor where, behind a closed door, she found the box-room.

There were rubbed leather cases and cabin trunks, ancient tennis racquets, stacks of pictures in tarnished frames—turned to the room as if someone had been looking at them and not turned them back. There were rusty skates, a side-saddle and an old-fashioned alpenstock, but there was also a wetsuit and a pair of metal skis. One would expect the old things to be in the farther reaches of the room, the modern equipment to hand. This wasn't so. In a dim corner near the window was a gleam of colour, almost fluorescent. It was a nylon rucksack. She started to work her way through to the corner.

When she came out of the box-room she walked back to the landing and paused. Through the staircase window she caught sight of the fog stealing under the headland on the far side of the bay. The top window blocked the sky but the sea was grey in the cloud shadow. She hesitated—and on the ground floor a door closed, very quietly.

She went down the stairs and along the stone passage. Light at the end showed that the kitchen door was open, but that to the dairy was closed.

'Mr Pryce!' she called loudly and without urgency, 'Come here. I left this door open—' she depressed the thumb latch, '—Who closed it?' Her tone was authoritative as she switched on the light.

The opening door encountered an obstacle. Carter stepped round the edge of it: a shocking sight with the light reflected from the steel of a chef's knife in his hand.

'It's not the only one in Abersaint,' she said emptily, unable to take her eyes off the wicked blade.

'It's the only one with blood on it.' He looked past her. 'Pryce isn't here. You're alone.'

'I can't see any blood.'

'It'll show under analysis.'

'You're guessing.'

He followed as she retreated to the front door and stepped out on the lawn. The air struck chill under the trees.

'Why are they all protecting her?' he asked. 'Even you.'

She took the question at its face value. 'The family is doing it out of loyalty; for my part, it's a sense of justice. You know about that, but you're blinded by grief.'

He flinched. 'You never thought—' he began, but she was tense, listening.

'There's a car coming.'

'That'll be the police.'

She nodded and walked round the side of

277

the house to the shrubbery. They saw a car pass the end of the tunnel and heard it stop in the yard. Doors slammed. A fist hammered on wood. A man shouted.

They moved forward and parted the leaves to see two uniformed men taking pick axes and shovels from the boot of a car. Miss Pink and Carter looked at each other with hard smiles.

She climbed the wooded bank behind the coach-house where the fog was caught in the branches: a strange dry fog, very thin at this altitude; now and again the sun managed to break through and then it was as hot as an oven. Below her, she saw Carter cross the yard and enter the house carrying the knife.

Traversing the fields she found herself in a fluid world of alternating cloud and colour. Trails like white smoke drifted along the banks and through gateways and between them the grass was brilliant and the cattle gaudy: red and white, black and white, yellow—then a wave rolled by and the beasts became grazing ghosts. Above it all, untouched and radiant, the mountain brooded with the angles of the fort etched against a gentian sky.

The land was so still and the cloud so mobile that distinction was blurred in the mind, even in the eye, and Miss Pink had the feeling, as the mist passed and the gaunt rock showed above braken on shadowless slopes, that there was movement on the scree.

Then she was wrapped in cloud again and the cromlech crouched like a malignant being beside the path and she, who had never found ancient monuments anything else but interesting, edged past it like a wary colt.

Even the banks were moving, the earth banks friezed with flowers, but this she thought, was rabbits, deceived by the gloom, come out for what they fancied was the evening feed. There was a smell too: a tang of scorching, but that would have been present throughout the summer as the cliff grass shrivelled in the heat; there was no wonder that the smell of it should drift inland on a south-west wind. Actually there was no wind, only the suggestion of air currents and that was suggested because the fog moved—yet it seemed to move of its own volition.

She had passed the cattle and was crossing the last field when things like big lizards came streaking through the fog, one to each side of her, staying just on the edge of her vision, curving behind her to merge and approach as one animal. As she turned to face them she distinguished two pairs of pricked ears and she wondered why dogs should be creeping with flat bellies as if they were shepherding when there was only herself in sight.

They advanced with closed mouths and without sound, making no overt threat, but their intention was clear. She turned aside and walked at right angles to her previous line, the dogs guiding her as they would guide a sheep. She came to a gate and the collies sank to the ground while she opened it. On the other side the Pritchards waited, grinning toothily.

'I smelled your smoke.' She addressed Mrs Pritchard who was holding the ubiquitous cigarette between stained fingers. 'I thought someone had started a fire. What do you want from me?'

Avril said: 'Mr Roderick and the rest of them is at Pentref.'

'And you want me to join them. Why?'

'*She* said so.' Mrs Pritchard pulled on her cigarette and her fingers trembled.

'Why should Rachel want me at Pentref? Is she there too?'

They made small movements of indecision. 'That's right,' Avril said. 'She's there with the others.'

'All the others?' Miss Pink stared at Pritchard who wouldn't meet her eyes. 'And the police,' she pressed. 'Where are they?'

'They're searching the top,' Mrs Pritchard said eagerly.

'Moving which way?'

Her husband motioned from west to east. If this were correct the police were moving away from Pentref, away from the Bowens—but not all the Bowens. Someone was not at Pentref.

She said firmly, in a tone that brooked no argument: 'There are others coming along behind me; go back and guide them through the fields.'

'But them don't need guiding,' Avril protested. Her mother pulled the girl's sleeve and the three of them moved away, the dogs at their heels.

Miss Pink went in the opposite direction, towards the cliffs where the air felt fresher and hinted of space. She heard voices before she saw anyone and she stood still beside a stunted thorn, straining her ears and watching. Figures loomed, moved, faded. Men grumbled prosaically and sticks thrashed the gorse. She heard Pryce cry savagely: 'What the hell's the use of that, man! Part the bushes carefully; if you beat them down, you're only covering up what we're looking for.'

They drifted past, so indistinct that she

couldn't tell which one was Pryce. When they had disappeared from sight she followed cautiously, her distance from them determined by the sound of their voices. Below, on the right, the unseen sea lay under the terrible slope but the police kept well back from the edge, combing the heath where the gorse bushes stood huge and misshapen and not like gorse at all.

Ahead she heard sharp exclamations as the searchers came to the top of the funnel where the strip of safe ground fined down to a few inches on the outside of the new fence. She saw shadows lift and drop and realised that they were climbing the stile to reach the enclosed field.

She let them go and then moved forward. The heath stopped on the edge of space and although there was an abyss beneath her she had the feeling that it wasn't empty.

Now she could hear the whisper of the sea and very distantly a soft chuckle that might have been a bird or possibly a motor muffled in the fog. There were other sounds: the click of a stone in the funnel, the thud of a rabbit's leg on turf. The gorse was moving, but that was impossible for nothing could move gorse except a gale—perhaps someone had left a gate open and one of the cows was on the cliff top. She wondered why the gulls were so quiet.

She felt somnolent, almost apathetic, drained. She had no sense of involvement in anything that was happening, but was anything happening? Surely only a vivid imagination allied with the incidence of the fog hinted that all along the cliffs something was holding its breath. But something *was* happening; there was an increase in sound, in the distinction of separate sounds. There were sharper tones and, visually, sharper outlines. She looked up and saw the cloud move; she looked back across the funnel and saw a figure, the profile turned, not towards Miss Pink, but inland.

A bird called, the rabbits kicked, thud, thud, thud: rhythmical, approaching—not rabbits but running feet beating the hard-packed earth, and in front of the feet came the sound of stumbling, of tearing gasps.

Wire sang as a heavy body struck the fence. Something ran along the inside of the wire, found the stile, climbed it clumsily and stood on the brink of the funnel, staring downwards, grasping the fence with one hand.

The running feet had halted. Shapes showed in the field, spaced at intervals and stationary. The figure released the wire, crouched, and started to creep crabwise down the funnel, fingers tearing at the grass like the claws of a desperate cat. Above, the others advanced, still in that careful formation and, without pausing, they started down the funnel.

They passed from sight and out of the depths came a scream, then a man's shout of alarm, and then the long slithering sound, decreasing as it descended, of something that did not thud and bound like a rock but retained contact with the grass. There was a moment's silence, then all the gulls rose crying out of the cove.

Cloud rolled up the funnel and Miss Pink stared down at a whirl of birds. The slopes weren't empty; a few yards below, Norman Kemp stood on the black scree tip, his shoulders hunched to his ears, his hands clutching at his face. There was no one else in the depression and no one on either side except, on her own level across the gap, that other figure, watching her husband as if she were unable to do anything else.

She walked round the rim. 'Who went down the gully?' she asked.

'Didn't you see? It was Iris.'

People came crashing through the gorse. They heard Pryce cry testily: 'Well, *I* heard it!'

They turned to face the police but as Pryce approached, red-faced and angry, their attention was jerked back to Norman who was shouting from below.

'What's he say?' Pryce glared at the gesticulating figure, hating every aspect of this: the dangerous ground, the wild panic of the birds, the boat in which the occupants were adding to the confusion, waving and pointing at the cliffs.

'What happened?' he asked. 'Who screamed?'

'It was Iris MacNally,' Miss Pink told him. She looked into Rachel's cool eyes. 'She was running in front of the rescue team. She couldn't have realised how steep the ground is here and she stared down the gully.'

Pryce stared at her blankly. 'The rescue team isn't here yet.'

Rachel said smoothly: 'The fog's deceptive; it was the cattle chasing her. Iris is terrified of cows.'

Miss Pink looked away. Pryce said: 'What's he doing down there?'

Norman was scrambling up the side of the funnel. He stumbled through the anthills and threw himself on Pryce.

'Do something!' he shouted. 'For Christ's

sake, do something!'

'The boat's there,' Pryce countered. 'We can't do anything up here, man. That's her only chance: the boat.'

But Norman seemed unable to reason. He turned on his wife. 'You! Go down there—' He broke off and his eyes darkened momentarily. 'You pushed her,' he said softly. Miss Pink moved to Rachel's side. The girl was expressionless.

'Shout to them!' He was raving again, this time at Miss Pink. 'Look! They're holding off! They're watching her drown.' He waved frantically towards the sea, screaming: 'Go in! Go in and pull her out!'

'They can't, Norman,' Rachel said quietly.

'What!'

'There's wire under the water; it's holding her down.'

He gave a choked cry and lurched forward. Pryce made a grab at him, jerking his head at his men.

'Help me get him into the field. You go first,' he said grimly to Rachel. 'Williams!'

The sergeant stepped forward and waited for Rachel to precede him to the stile. As Miss Pink followed and held back for Williams to edge along the grass clutching the fence, she saw the Bowens and Samuel coming along the heath from the west, Roderick hobbling ahead.

'What's happening over there?' he barked. 'What's the trouble with the boat?'

No one answered; they were all occupied with reaching the safety of the field. From the inland side of it Carter and the Pritchards were hurrying towards them. No one said anything; it was as if each person waited for someone else to break the silence. Then Carter came up and for him only one person existed. He stared at Rachel with cold hatred.

'There's blood in the kitchen,' he said.

Rachel sighed. Pryce exclaimed: 'My men didn't tell you that.'

'They didn't have to.'

Norman broke in quickly: 'It was an accident. The clothes rack fell down. He was struggling and she had the knife in her hand. He was blackmailing her. And she—'

'She was with me!' Doreen confronted him, whitefaced. 'She's been protecting you all along, she'd have done anything for you; she even confessed—'

Norman drew a shuddering breath. 'Crazy,' he breathed: 'Stark, bloody crazy. I wasn't even Sandra's lover.' He turned to Pryce eagerly: 'It was only a quarrel between two girls; she hit her with the first thing that

287

came to hand. It was manslaughter, wasn't it? She'll get off. It was the same thing with Jakey: a sudden uncontrollable impulse. She's on drugs you see: drugs and drink, that's what it was. It was all a series of tragic mistakes; I never realised how far it had gone in her mind. I could have stopped Jakey's death that evening if I'd been quick enough.'

Miss Pink glanced at Rachel. The girl's eyelids drooped.

'But why are you so adamant,' she asked curiously. 'Rachel can't testify against you, and Iris is dead.'

He grinned horribly and tossed back his yellow hair with a reflex gesture. 'That,' he said, with a catch in his breath, 'I'll find hard to forgive.'

'But surely the person who wanted to kill Iris would be the person who tortured her?' His eyes were suddenly blank, searching hers. 'Stretched out on the kitchen table,' she said, 'covered with burns, and the poker in the fire.'

He'd seen the trap and he smiled boyishly. 'That was an hallucination. The drugs, you know.'

Miss Pink withdrew her hand from her pocket and extended it towards him. He looked at what lay on her palm, shrank back, turned and charged the men behind him, between him and the stile.

'Stop him!' Pryce shouted.

They held him. At sight of their appalled faces he shrieked: 'It wasn't me, I swear it! It was her idea from the beginning: the fire, and Jakey—she didn't *plan* Jakey, that was unexpected, but she killed him all right. I just took the body. . . .' His eye fell on Roderick. 'Even you! She put the branch there; she meant you to be killed. It was the money; she'd do anything for money.'

Roderick made a gesture of disgust. 'You're mad. The money was hers. It's all to come to her. Yer can't even tell a good lie.'

'He's not lying,' Miss Pink said. 'He's talking about Iris.'

CHAPTER SEVENTEEN

THE BROAD SCENE was one of confusion but individuals had themselves well in hand. On the edge of the crowd Rachel talked earnestly to Miss Pink, a knot of people surrounded Norman and herded him away, Pryce approached Roderick.

'We haven't taken those flags up in the kitchen. We have to now, of course.'

'Of course,' the old man murmured, and, with an attempt at levity: 'I'll expect them to be re-laid level.'

People started to drift away from the cliffs; they'd only been waiting for the police party to get a good start. Doreen and Rachel walked ahead deep in conversation. The rest of them walked as if dazed. Miss Pink was with Samuel. After a time he said: 'I'm thinking of my kitten: totally without viciousness—you know?'

'Don't forget the people: Rachel, her family, friends. They weren't vicious.'

'They make it worse: their suffering. And Sandra.'

'Don't opt out. You're going to be needed.'

They walked on, holding the gates politely

for each other. The cromlech squatted beside the path, massive and imposing even in the sunshine. Doreen turned back to them, her face drawn and anxious.

'Samuel, she wants to go home with you.'

'To my place?'

'Yes. She can't go to Riffli and she knows we'll be talking at the hotel. She can't face that. Take her home, please, Samuel.'

'Of course I will.'

He sped after the solitary figure at the other side of the field.

'A sensible solution to that problem,' Miss Pink remarked. 'He's a good friend.'

'Rupert says she ought to have married him, but it's always been platonic. He's much too old, of course, but perhaps that's what she needs: an older man.' Miss Pink said nothing. 'You'll come back to the hotel,' Doreen stated, but diffidently. 'If you're not too tired. . . .'

*　　　*　　　*

Rupert and Doreen, Roderick and Miss Pink were in the sitting room at the hotel. On a coffee table lay the object which Miss Pink had shown to Norman Kemp. It was about four inches square: a piece of flesh-coloured

291

plastic with a bubbly black splodge in the middle. The Bowens regarded it with blank faces. Miss Pink placed it on her bare arm.

'Burn!' Roderick gasped. 'A third degree burn. Where d'yer find it?'

'In the box-room at Riffli. Someone had been in there recently and that attracted my attention. Besides, I had an idea what to look for by then.'

'There's a batch of 'em: plastic wounds for First Aid exercises. Verisimilitude. What's it got ter do with this business, eh?'

'I know,' Doreen said, staring at the plastic patch with revulsion. '*That* was Rachel's nightmare. You tell them, Melinda; I can't trust myself.'

'This nightmare—or hallucination—' Miss Pink said grimly, '—was the sight of Iris supposedly being tortured with a red-hot poker. My showing the burn to him broke Norman because Rachel never told me at the time that Norman was in the kitchen with Iris and he was putting the poker in the fire. In other words, he was the torturer. That's why she came rushing down to the village; there was no one left in Riffli to appeal to.'

'I don't understand,' Rupert protested. 'You mean Iris had some of those objects stuck on her. . . . A trick? Why?'

292

'Some time before this happened, Rachel saw something else, and she told Iris. She was shocked but by this time she had doubts about her own state of mind so Iris was able to convince her that it was an hallucination, and she got her to bed and gave her brandy and tranquillisers. But she was too strung up for them to have much effect and some time later when she heard a scream downstairs she went down to investigate. The kitchen door was locked so she went out in the yard and looked through a window. The light was on. You know what she saw.'

'Go on,' Roderick ordered.

'What was the other thing she saw?' Doreen asked tightly. 'The first thing?'

'She saw Jakey's body in the freezer. She'd been in her bedroom and the drawing room all evening. Norman and Iris said they were watching T.V. in the dining room; that was a concocted alibi. We don't know yet what time Jakey arrived at Riffli but for part of the time they'd be frantically clearing up after killing him. No one was in the dining room. Rachel must have been upstairs when Jakey was killed. She got restless and went to talk to Iris but on her way to the kitchen she saw that the dairy door was open. She looked inside, thinking Iris would be there, saw the freezer lid

293

wasn't closed properly and went to see what was stopping it. Literally she couldn't believe what she saw. She walked in the kitchen and found Iris washing the floor.'

'And asked Iris what the body was doing in the freezer,' Doreen put in. 'And Iris acted the good old earth mother and got her to bed. I see.'

'Which of them killed Jakey?' Rupert asked loudly.

'You heard Norman on the cliff,' Miss Pink reminded him. 'He wouldn't have made that up. When he said *she* let the clothes rack down on Jakey, he was referring to Iris. Doreen misinterpreted that and rushed in with the first lie that came to mind. Norman saw her mistake and saw a chance to inculpate Rachel. That doesn't matter. What does matter is the method of the murder. The clothes rack was empty when Samuel and I arrived at Riffli with Rachel. Letting it down on Jakey and stabbing him through the clothes would account for there being no blood on anyone. There'd be plenty on the clothes of course, on Jakey's shirt and on the floor. So she washed the floor, burned the floor cloth and all the stained clothes. That cooker was going at full blast when we arrived. It takes a long time to burn a pile of clothing.'

'What part did Norman play in this?' Roderick barked. 'Did he take the body to the cliffs?'

'He must have done. Perhaps he put it in the woods after Iris told him Rachel had seen it in the freezer. Probably he took it to the shaft much later at night, after we'd left Riffli and you and Rachel had gone to bed. That was when he would have put the clothes on the beach too.'

Doreen said: 'So the purpose of that ghastly charade with the burns was to convince Rachel she'd had an hallucination and so she'd believe the body in the freezer was imagination too?' She looked at Miss Pink coldly. 'I wish she'd lived; I wish I'd got my hands on her.'

'Why did she kill Jakey?' Roderick asked.

'He was blackmailing her. She killed Sandra.'

'It wasn't Norman then?'

'They were working together. She must have killed Sandra because Norman had to be the one who made the telephone call imitating the local police.'

'You've lost me,' Rupert said.

'Do yer know the whole story, Mel?'

'Most of it.'

'Did it start with that attempt on me life?'

'That was the first thing.'

'You knew, right from the start, that someone tried to kill Dad?' Rupert was belligerent.

'Oh no; at the start I held the same opinion as you: that Roderick's imagination had run away with him—' the old man shot her a resentful glance, '—I was worried though, because I knew there was a sadist loose in the village; I'd seen Jakey roll a rock down the funnel, just to frighten me, and Rachel gave me a graphic description of the boy. But if the branch had been put on the steps deliberately, at that time I attributed it to mindless hooliganism, not to a plot. And it was ousted from my mind as other things occurred. They started to happen at your party, Roderick, although I knew before the party that Rachel hated Sandra.'

Doreen stirred. 'Small wonder at that.'

'Yes.' Miss Pink's tone lacked conviction. 'At the party Sandra became very indiscreet and mentioned her book—'

'But we know all this,' Rupert interrupted. 'We want to know why Sandra was killed.'

'Let Mel tell it,' Roderick growled.

'As I see it, sweetie,' Doreen said, 'she was murdered because of the book.'

'The book disappeared,' Miss Pink conceded, 'so we thought it was the motive for the first murder. Actually it had no importance; probably it was burned in the fire. At the same time it was its disappearance, and the absence of Thorne and the Spitfire, that first roused suspicion—that and the fact that Sandra wasn't drunk when the television men left the cottage, couldn't have been drunk when the fire started, yet had made no attempt even to get up from the bed. I don't think accident was implied so much by the presence of the bottle and the lighter in the debris, as murder—and murder by Thorne. Iris had guessed he wouldn't stay to face the police and she guessed correctly. What she didn't bargain for was Jakey Jones staying behind after the party at the mill cottage. Why he stayed is anyone's guess; Thorne had caught him once doing a Peeping Tom act. But he saw something that night; perhaps he was lurking in the woods and he realised that someone else was there; a young boy would be quieter in bushes than Iris. And, being Jakey, if he knew someone else was keeping a watch on the cottage, he'd hang around and try to find out why. He certainly saw Iris; perhaps he saw her enter the cottage after Thorne left. And he knew—or guessed—what happened inside; why otherwise should he go to school next day, leaving on the school bus at eight-thirty when the television men didn't report the fire until after nine? Ossie Hughes says he was subdued all day, and then talked about getting money from someone when they came home to the village. Then he disappeared.

'But that day, before Jakey talked to me about money, I'd talked to Rachel. A curious thing happened there: a sudden change of mood. At first she was very sensible—and she wasn't in the least morbid. And she seemed to accept quite calmly that Norman had been attracted to Sandra. But later I mentioned the time of the fire and that Norman had been working in the coach-house and Iris watching television in the kitchen. At that point Rachel flew off the handle and wildly tried to incriminate Tony Thorne. She called him a sacrificial lamb.'

'Why did she change?' Roderick asked. 'Because she knew Norman—no, you said Iris killed Sandra.'

'Both of them. What's important is that they alibied each other. I told Rachel the fire started before eleven-thirty. She'd gone to bed around ten. She woke, thought it was very late, and Norman hadn't come to bed. She was used to that. She went down to make herself a cup of tea, only to find lights everywhere and the television going in the kitchen. It was eleven-fifteen. Obsessed with the idea that Norman was with Sandra, she put no significance on the absence of Iris. She returned to bed and when Norman came up after midnight, she said nothing. She told me she was sick of scenes. It wasn't until she learned the time the fire started, and when I told her that Norman said he never left Riffli that evening, that she started to see a connection. Eventually she came to remember that Iris was also missing but she assumed the woman had gone to bed and left the television on, perhaps for Norman to watch. And if Iris says she watched until very late, then she was protecting Norman and therefore an ally. You have to remember that Rachel was very confused at this time.'

'Did you say she was used to Norman coming to bed late?' Doreen asked. 'Where was he then?'

'With Iris.'

'Iris! Under the same roof? Oh no, not Iris.'

'You saw him on the cliffs. She was dead and he was devastated. He turned on his wife.' They were silent, remembering. 'So,' she went on, 'Rachel protected Norman, and you all protected her. As anyone would have

299

done,' she added smoothly, 'particularly in view of her bizarre behaviour the night Jakey was killed: the so called hallucination of Iris being tortured. The thought of a black-out, or black-outs due to drugs and drink, crossed my mind. What else could it be? And then, the following morning, I met Carter—'

'Yes, who *is* Carter?' asked Doreen.

She told them, and she told them the story he'd recounted at Captain's Cottage. 'Why should he come down here with such a tale if it were untrue? If he thought Thorne had murdered Sandra and stolen the typescript, he would have gone after Thorne. Carter seemed to me to be a man who had nothing to lose, in his way an honest man, but utterly ruthless: a man bent on revenge. And the story fitted. There was the place where the Spitfire could have been parked, the telephone nearby, rising ground from which Norman could have signalled to Iris and vice versa. I've no doubt Norman will confess in order to save his own skin. He's broken already, only the details are left. My guess is that he drove the Spitfire away from the cottage as the reporters were leaving. At ten-thirty or thereabouts it would be dark enough that no one would pay any attention. The reporters weren't sober anyway. Iris would be hidden in the woods waiting for the last car to leave. Even if Thorne had gone to the door with the television men and seen that the Spitfire was missing, what would have happened? The T.V. men would hardly have stayed to help him find it; the assumption would be that a reporter had taken it for fun. The T.V. men would have left, and Thorne stayed fuming in the cottage. It's very doubtful that he would have rung the police. Now I wonder if Iris knew that he had a record?

'But he didn't come to the door. Iris would then signal to Norman that there was no one at the cottage except Thorne and Sandra. It was a pre-arranged signal; a flash would be enough. She had only to climb the bank of the stream to be within sight of that rising ground above the main road. It may have been that signal Jakey saw; it would have whetted his appetite.

'When Norman saw the signal, he put through the call purporting to come from the police. When Thorne left, Iris went into the cottage, knocked Sandra out, took the typescript—I feel sure that there would have been a key to the filing cabinet in Sandra's handbag—and set the fire. They both returned to Riffli, Iris by way of the stepping stones across the river. I found

Avril Pritchard obliterating the prints this morning.'

'The Pritchards are in this?' Roderick exclaimed.

'Avril did it for Rachel who thought Norman had made the prints. Everyone covering up like mad, you see, but one person threatening exposure: Jakey. He was sharp, but not sharp enough, and he was conceited. He'd got away with all his mischief to date. I remember feeling completely frustrated at one point. What could one do with a boy like that? If he'd been caught for a comparatively minor offence and sent to Borstal, he'd have come out worse than he went in. No, Jakey was heading for disaster; his mother knew that.

'When I found Rachel hiding in the cavern I played it that way: that Jakey was dead. I was led to do it by her "confession". What she told me was a string of lies and omissions but they were telling me more than I'd have got from her with point-blank questions, so I told her about Jakey's clothes being found. She assumed that his body would turn up shortly, and she assured me that he was dead before he was put in the water—'

'But he wasn't in the water!' Rupert said.

'And that was the clincher—for me,' Miss

Pink continued. 'She knew he was dead, but not where his body was. There was a lot she didn't know. Thorne never mentioned to Carter that the typescript was on Sandra's bed but Rachel, assuming it played some part in the affair, said she was reading it. She also said she hit Sandra with a candlestick. That was significant. A brandy bottle was found near the bed and could have been the weapon to knock her unconscious. But only the killer would have known what weapon was used. Rachel saw my question as a trap, remembered that some brandy bottles are flask-shaped and not handy weapons, so she made a wild guess at an alternative. But the glaring omission in that false confession was any mention of the telephone call to Fleet Street that brought the reporters flocking to the mill cottage.'

'I'd forgotten about that,' Roderick said. 'Didn't the agent—this Carter feller. . . . No, that was what was assumed at the time.'

'Rachel's not mentioning it recalled it to my mind. By this time, you see, I was almost certain that Norman was the killer but what part did that call play? It wasn't made by anyone who feared exposure from the book because they were drawing attention to it. Sandra and Thorne found the sudden publicity embarrassing. Could the motive have been to drive them away? Pryce thought so. It was after Sandra announced her intention of staying that she was killed. Then I remembered Waterhouse, one of the reporters, telling me that the person who made the call to the Press said Sandra was known in London as Cynthia Gale. The only people who knew she was writing a book were at your party, Roderick. Thorne knew but he was discounted when Jakey's body was found. When the boy was killed Thorne was in custody. But who was at the party who knew Sandra as Cynthia Gale?'

'You're presuming someone else besides Norman,' Roderick said. 'How did yer tumble to Iris?'

'Caradoc went back to the kitchen and told Thirza Jones and Iris about the book and the two women went round to the front of the house and saw Sandra through the drawing room windows. That was the first time Iris saw Sandra. She made that telephone call. And next day Roderick told you, Doreen, that he'd have Sandra at Riffli and ask her to leave. Was Iris waiting on you at tea-time?'

'She was,' Doreen said. 'Anyway the door would have been open in that heat. She was the sort of person who listened at doors.'

Rupert said, frowning: 'You seem to have jumped a bit. How did you decide it was Iris who made the call to Fleet Street?'

'Elimination,' Miss Pink said. 'Think of the other people who were present at Roderick's party. Roderick couldn't have killed Sandra; he was immobilised on the night she died.'

'But,' Doreen broke in, 'you were looking for Norman's accomplice.'

'Yes. And the killers didn't take a car to the mill cottage. They walked there and back. There was yourself.' She shrugged. 'I could not see you working with Norman. There was Samuel: highly unlikely from what I knew of him but he couldn't be eliminated. There was Rachel who, unless she were a genius at acting, told too many lies to be the killer. Rupert had an alibi for the time of Jakey's murder. Caradoc and Thirza wouldn't have murdered their own son. There was only Iris left. She saw Sandra but couldn't risk Sandra's seeing herself. First she tried to drive the girl away, then she killed her.'

'Why couldn't she risk being seen?' Rupert asked.

'One hundred thousand pounds.' Miss Pink was a trifle smug.

'What's that supposed ter mean?'

'The value of your estate.'

'Possibly. No one's selling it. And I'm not dead yet.'

'You nearly were.'

'Ah. Who put that branch on the granary steps?'

'Norman I would think: at Iris's bidding.'

'But then the estate would go to Rachel—and she'd never sell.'

'Suppose she committed suicide, or had an accident on the cliffs?'

They gaped at her.

'Norman!' Doreen hissed. 'He'd have done that?'

'How many husbands have killed their wives for money? He's had a hand in two murders already, and an attempt on Roderick. When he confesses, or rather when he elaborates what he said on the cliffs, he's going to state a motive. Did you never think that he married Rachel for her money?' Doreen nodded assent. 'And when they came to Abersaint, Iris left the hotel and went to Riffli. She was a very managing woman and Norman relied on her completely. In any conversation with the two of them he turned to her, literally, when he was at a loss. He was dominated by her, and she wanted that money. The nuclear power campaign would have given her the idea. Another site had been chosen but she would bank on the Energy Authority coming back. This site would be kept in mind for the future. Then Norman would sell and the couple would disappear. Perhaps,' she added thoughtfully, 'Norman would really disappear, leaving Iris with a fortune.'

'She'd kill him too?' Rupert gasped.

'Look at her record.'

'Where does Sandra come in?' Roderick asked. 'How did her presence here threaten Iris?'

Miss Pink nodded slowly. 'Was there something in Iris's past that would make Sandra speculate as to what the woman was doing down here working as a housekeeper to a man who was very rich?' She didn't add 'and very old'.

The telephone rang. Doreen got up and answered it.

'It's Pryce,' she said to Miss Pink. 'He wants to speak to you.'

Miss Pink crossed the room and took the receiver. The conversation was enigmatic. She said 'yes' several times then asked: 'Did Iris MacNally have a record? . . . I see. Thank you for ringing. Yes, I'll be there later.'

She sat down again.

307

'He's confessed. It was the money. They're working on a statement. Iris has no record under that name, it seems, but the body's been recovered and, of course, there'll be the fingerprints. Norman says Sandra was killed because she knew Iris. Pryce isn't satisfied with that but he's not worried. He wants to get those fingerprints. He said he'd ring again. Where's Carter?'

No one knew.

'I don't want to see him again,' Doreen said. 'He started all this with his wretched book.'

'Not at all.' Miss Pink was firm. 'The plot was there already. If Sandra hadn't arrived in Abersaint, Roderick was in line to be murdered, and then Rachel.'

'There were victims though.' Roderick was morose. 'Sandra and Jakey.'

'We could spare one of those,' Rupert said darkly.

'But not the other.' Miss Pink stood up. 'I have to find Carter.'

CHAPTER EIGHTEEN

SHE FOUND HIM sooner than she expected. He was sitting on a bench on the quay, staring across the basin that was filling with the tide. Lights were on in the cottages and the bats were out. It was a lovely night. She crossed the quay and sat down beside him.

'I was waiting for you,' he said. He sounded inordinately tired.

She listened to the water lapping against the moored boats.

'Will you take a message to Mrs Kemp?'

'Yes.'

'Ask her to forgive me.'

'I'll do that, Mr Carter. May I offer you my sympathy?'

'That's very kind of you. I was, as you said, blind. She was very dear to me. I hoped. . . . Do you know why she was killed?'

She told him about the plot to gain possession of Riffli. He was silent for a while and then he said: 'I've known a lot of criminals: ones who were caught, and the others who got away with it. You'd say they've got no morals but they all have some touch of humanity: good family men, fair employers—sometimes

309

ruthless, but none without some kind of code. But of all the people I've known I've never met anyone truly evil. Except her.'

She turned on him. 'If you knew her, why didn't you say so? Why go after Rachel?'

'I didn't know she was here. I never saw her. But I've seen the body. Her name was Eileen Jotti.'

Someone was sculling across the water: a dark shape slipping through the reflections.

'She was married to a Moroccan,' he went on, 'now doing time for the only gang murder, the only murder they could pin on him: a very nasty one. He got fifteen years. Some of his gang were sent down with him, not all of them by any means. The rest of them will be looking for Eileen—your Iris MacNally. She shopped them.'

'Why?' Miss Pink asked. 'She didn't get anything out of it, judging by appearances.'

'She stayed on the outside; that would have been the reward for shopping them. And then Jotti was a big man in London; he had a lot of irons in the fire. Porn shops and strip clubs were only the legal side; he was an importer—of heroin. He had links all over Europe. He wouldn't have been caught, except for Eileen. She'd have meant to take over the business but Jotti didn't trust her.

He made other arrangements and Eileen was squeezed out. One moment she was the boss's wife, the next: nothing, and there was a contract out for her. Jotti knew who shopped him all right. So she came here, on the run. She'd have been to other places first, never staying long in one place, always looking for an opening. But at her time of life she'd be tired of running—and the stakes were high here. In South America she could set herself up in the brothel business with a hundred thousand. She was a madame when she met Jotti. I've seen Sandra in some of Jotti's clubs. She'd been a stripper.'

'And Sandra would have talked about her when she went back to London. No wonder. . . .'

'If only she'd rung me—but I was abroad. In any case, she didn't *know*. Eileen Jotti got to her and she never had a hint of the danger.'

Softly across the water came the strains of music.

'He likes Haydn,' Carter murmured. 'I've been in the churchyard. His kitten was there. It came to me.'

He stood up. 'Now I'm going to headquarters and see what I can do for Thorne. An unlikeable chap, but he's done nothing wrong—here.'

Miss Pink stood beside him. 'I hope all goes well with you, Mr Carter.'

He raised his hand in salute and walked away to the cars. Along the quay there were lights in the big police trailer. She drove to her cottage and, entering the living room, slumped in a chair, feeling tired and sad.

There was a knock at the window and Samuel's moon-face showed on the other side of the glass.

'Come on over,' he said as she opened it. 'Rachel told me to fetch you. We heard your car.'

'What does she want to talk about?' she asked as they went along the terrace.

'I don't know.' He was evasive. 'You've been a long time with the others.'

She stopped on the other side of the stile.

'We were working it out. Pryce rang to say that Norman's confessed. There was a plot to sell the estate.'

'Yes.' He wasn't surprised. 'We've been talking about that.'

They threaded their way through the tombstones, the grass dewy against their legs. Caithness was waiting on the wall, silhouetted against the light.

'He won't go beyond the patio now,' Samuel said. 'He's got a thing about gulls.'

'He did. Carter was in the graveyard earlier and Caithness went to him.'

'That's nice. Carter ought to have a cat.'

They descended a short ladder to the patio. Rachel came to the french window. From behind her came the strains of a Haydn concerto.

'Good,' she said calmly, 'I'm glad you came.'

'I have a message for you from Mr Carter. He asks your forgiveness.'

'Oh, poor man.'

Samuel turned off the music and they sat down. Rachel looked broodingly at Miss Pink.

'It was because of the money, wasn't it?'

'Yes. He's confessed.'

'It had to be. I'm afraid he married me under false pretences. He thought I was very rich, you see.'

'He couldn't have been so badly off himself: managing a hotel.'

'He was the barman.'

Samuel avoided Miss Pink's eye.

'I told people he was the manager,' Rachel went on. 'He'd have been embarrassed otherwise. It was a shock to him when he arrived at Riffli; he'd expected a grand mansion with staff, and Grandad running a Rolls. I—hadn't given him the details. He knew what the land was worth, of course, and that it would come to me, but he didn't understand how I felt about it until he met Grandad and saw how things were. He realised there wasn't a hope of selling. We had rows about it. About other things too. People didn't know the half of it.' She looked at Samuel.

'I'm sure Miss Pink understands,' he said. 'There's no need to go over it again; you're only hurting yourself.'

Rachel picked at the cover of her chair.

'You all thought I was going barmy.'

'No, we didn't—'

'I thought so myself.' She passed a hand over her forehead, then looked fiercely at Miss Pink. 'Sam's right; you don't want to hear it all. I'll tell you quick—' her voice was hard, '—we quarrelled, I'd have a drink; he said I was turning into an alcoholic, but he started dropping hints—about Sandra. Then he'd say I was possessive, demanding. He'd come to bed in the small hours and tell me he'd been out walking, but he'd smile when he said it. . . . I went on tranquillisers. It was a kind of downwards spiral, you know? I couldn't get hold of anything.'

'I know.' Miss Pink was placid. 'It's not a unique situation. I've seen it before.'

'You have!'

'She wasn't that bad,' Samuel put in. 'It was Norman who said she was.'

'I puzzled that out,' Miss Pink said. 'People were saying "Norman tells me" or "Norman says". The worst parts always seemed to emanate from Norman. Wasn't it he told you that some prehistoric peoples practised cannibalism?'

'Yes. He found it in one of Grandad's books and showed it to me. He kept on about it; he found it fascinating.'

'That's why I couldn't find a relevant book on your shelves.'

'It was a campaign to make her morbid.' Samuel was furious. 'And we all fell for it. I'm sorry, love; you don't want to go on with this, do you?'

'You can't believe what a relief it is to get everything clear. And to think that I used to turn to Iris!'

'She was far the worst of the two,' Miss Pink said.

'I know. He was just weak and greedy. And she was so kind that night—' her voice dropped, '—she put me to bed, and then she covered herself with those awful things—'

'Look—' Samuel began.

'All right.' She resumed her hard tone. 'So I thought I was barmy and I ran away and hid

315

in the cavern—I'm glad you didn't believe me when I said there were no ledges inside—I *was* going mad there on my own. But when you told me Jakey was dead, I knew it hadn't been an hallucination: seeing his body in the freezer, so neither was the other thing: Iris being burned. It was a trick. And Iris was involved. I wasn't staying in that cavern any longer when I knew I was sane—and I wanted to get Iris.'

'Why did you send Avril to cover the tracks by the river?'

'I thought Norman killed Sandra but if they were working it between them, then I was certain Iris was the dominant one. I knew her, you see.'

The telephone rang. Samuel answered it.

'Pryce wants to speak to you, Miss Pink.'

She took the receiver.

Pryce said: 'I thought you'd be there when I couldn't get you at your place. We're getting a clear picture now.' His voice droned on, telling her nothing new. 'Kemp's intent on saving his own skin,' he ended.

'Have you seen Carter?' she asked.

'I'm going to see him now. I understand he has something to tell me about Eileen Jotti.' He waited for her reaction. 'Jotti. Remember him: the gang boss in London?'

'Carter told me.'

'Oh.' He was disappointed, then he revived with a dry chuckle. 'Kemp's raving again.'

'What do you mean?'

'I was questioning him about her fall. Know what he said?'

'What?'

'Said she was being followed down the gully by a lot of men *in skins*! Walking upright, he said. On that ground! It won't wash, of course; they all try it on at the end, like Haigh saying he drank his victims' blood. He's going to try to plead insanity. Insanity my—Excuse me, ma'am. But he'll stand trial. He's as sane as you or me.'

'Marvellous: the things they get up to.'

She replaced the receiver carefully, sat down and gave them the gist of the information.

'What was that last bit about?' Samuel asked: 'The things they get up to?'

'Pryce reckons Norman's going for a plea of insanity. He maintains Iris was followed down the funnel by men in skins walking upright.'

Samuel got up and stalked round the room. He stopped on the hearth rug and stared at them.

'Is he mad after all? I mean, no sane person

317

would think men in skins would cop a plea of insanity. It's so puerile!'

Rachel smiled. 'I'm so glad there's no capital punishment because it's funny—isn't it, Miss Pink?' Her eyes clouded. 'Miss Pink—you do think it's funny?'

'What did you see?'

'No. You tell me what *you* saw. Please.'

Samuel looked from one to the other.

'What is this? You said the cattle were chasing Iris!'

Miss Pink said, watching Rachel intently: 'I heard running feet and I saw a line of figures spread out like a sweep search, and when she struck the fence they stopped and waited. When she climbed over the stile and started down the funnel they advanced again, walking.'

'Then what?' The girl's eyes were shadowed.

'They walked down the funnel like people walking down a gentle slope.'

'Did they bunch at the stile?'

'No,' Miss Pink said. 'They stayed spaced out.'

Samuel turned to Rachel. 'What did you see?'

'Exactly the same.'

'What, *people*? How did they cross the

fence?' They didn't help him. He stared at them, dumbfounded, then relaxed, became heartily masculine: a man humouring womenfolk.

'You both saw a line of men: a sweep search, like a rescue team, right?' They nodded. 'So they came to the fence and at that moment you were probably both watching Iris—'

'Well, I looked at Iris,' Miss Pink admitted.

'So did I.'

'And when you looked back the chaps were going down the funnel. But you can get over a fence easily if you're a young fit man: you put one hand on the fence post and vault over. And we all think the funnel is impassably steep, but very nimble climbers could get down there upright, couldn't they? It's not impossible. Well, couldn't they?'

'Perhaps,' Miss Pink conceded.

'And then the fog rolled away,' Rachel said, 'and there was no one in the funnel except Norman. I'm glad you saw them, Miss Pink.'

'It was the rescue team,' Samuel insisted. 'It'll all be explained tomorrow.'